Peter Money's books of poetry include hyl  ɔ
sequence with Saadi Youssef, *To day – mi*ɲ c
collaboration *Blue Square* (2007); *Che: A* d
a book of translations, with Sinan Antoon, ɔɩ ɯɪɛ ɪɯ— li
Youssef (2012). His most recent book is *American Drone: New and Select Poems* (2013). Money's other books include *These Are My Shoes* (1991), *A Big Yellow* (1996), *Between Ourselves* (1997), *Instruments* (1998), and *Finding It: Selected Poems* (2000). A co-founder of the literary journal *Writers' Bloc*, Money also founded the journals *Lame Duck* and *Across Borders*.

His poems have appeared in the *American Poetry Review*, the *Sun*, the *Berkeley Review*, the *Hawaii Review* and *Solo*, among others, and in the City Lights anthology *Days I Moved Through Ordinary Sound*, as well as on Garrison Keillor's "The Writer's Almanac". His work has been translated into Spanish in *Ultramar Literatura*. His "poem boxes" have been displayed and sold at the Berta Walker Gallery in Provincetown. In addition to his collaborative CD *Blue Square*, Money has collaborated with cartoonist Rick Veitch in "Beat Panels/Top Down."

He is the director of Harbor Mountain Press, and has taught at Lebanon College, where he guided the Associates in Creative Writing program. He was among the first faculty members at the pioneering Center For Cartoon Studies. A past poet-teacher for WritersCorps, the poetry in the schools program modelled on AmeriCorps, and a state judge for Poetry Out Loud, Money received a grass-roots nomination for the position of Vermont State Poet Laureate in 2011.

Peter performs with the band Los Lorcas.

PRAISE FOR *OH WHEN THE SAINTS*

"To say Peter Money's *Oh When The Saints* is beautifully written doesn't give this multi-faced, humane, and profoundly moving book justice. But damnit I'll say it. This book is beautifully written, from start to finish. There were so many times I simply re-read a sentence for the sheer joy of its cadence. Listen to this: 'How can a girl cultivate gladness after sorrow? Come flood, come drought, come storms of circumstance or unexpected pain, Kath made glad-rags from decimated suits.' A poet, a novelist, Money is the rare fusion. I savored the deeply felt human connections that animate this novel. May the Saint (and Denny, Kath, Nuala, and the others) live on."
—Peter Orner, author of *Love and Shame and Love*, and editor of *Underground America*

"Young Denny follows sounds and sensations in the hope of a bright future. A great city clutter has to be negotiated. Finding love is a small miracle. Keeping his eye to the kaleidoscope, Peter Money writes with artistry and invention."
—Philip Davison, author of *Eureka Dunes*

"Hyper-aware Denny, a young American in Dublin, makes his tentative way towards adulthood with a supporting cast of oddball friends. Denny hopes for a big love, the 'girl named Ireland'. Akin to a Joycean ramble, *Oh When the Saints* follows a sensitive boy on the reluctant verge of manhood, who cannot help endlessly analysing his own – and others' – place in the stream of life. His heart is 'a sack of air' until he meets a trainee librarian with ambitions to be wild. This is a strange, elliptical novel of ideas, told in punchy, poetic prose; Peter Money's is a vivid, fresh and welcome voice."
—Nuala O'Connor, author of *Joyride to Jupiter*

Oh When the Saints

First published in 2019 by
Liberties Press
1 Terenure Place | Terenure | Dublin 6W | Ireland
Tel: +353 (0) 86 853 8793
www.libertiespress.com

Distributed in the United States and Canada by
Casemate IPM | 1950 Lawrence Road | Havertown | Pennsylvania
19083 | USA
T: (610) 853 9131 | E: casemate@casematepublishers.com

Copyright © Peter Money
The author asserts his moral rights.
ISBN (print): 978-1-912589-02-9
ISBN (e-book): 978-1-912589-03-6

2 4 6 8 10 9 7 5 3 1
A CIP record for this title is available from the British Library.
Cover design by Roudy Design
Printed in Dublin by Sprint Print

To Neil,
who makes good
in the world.
I just know.

Oh When the Saints

My thanks, Israel.

Peter Money

LIB
ERT
IES

For Maura Keyes Naughton
and Joe Mernagh;

for Olivia, Eoghan, Niccolai, Lorcan, Eimear, Ashley,
and their friends.

And for Lorcan Collins, Sarah Stewart Taylor, Charlie O'Brien,
Maite, Naill, Jessica, James,

and Hartley, Lily and Lucinda, with enormous love,
– and to the parents of all of us,

family and friends
past present forward

&
for NB, MA, ML, MW, EB, TH, AS, MP, BJ, TF, TG, PH,
and for Sarah O'Sullivan, wherever she may be,
and, of course, for the Saint.

Chapter One

In Rathmines people left their houses and flats one by one, like a wall of sand beginning to break up with pressure behind it over time. The charity shops were closed for donations so someone had left a box in front of one of them. In an airport this wouldn't do. No one noticed the hand of a doll sticking out of the side of the box but Denny did. Commuters, gripers, strategists . . . .

The only music was the onerous strain of bus brakes, an echoed heel landing too square before the curb, a restrained four-cylinder engine in first and then second gear. The smell of diesel, a mixture of fish – maybe ambergris – and coal, bitters and sweets, boot leather and shaving lather. All this tactile and sensory stuff and Denny held onto a sense of being left behind.

Because he had little choice, to amuse himself he followed the sounds and sensations to their internal conclusions. If Denny could conjure *himself* as bus brakes he thought he felt indeed a hidden brute force. 'Grrrrrr. I am a man. A bull in stride. Bollocks to walls and if the walls had ears . . . .' He suddenly felt his own slight girth like the weight of an engine block rolling on wheels, held to a stop as if someone's flattened hands pushed against his bare chest as his eyes rolled back. As he stretched into a longer stride he was breathing a primordial leather that the canal opened up, a kind of intoxicant of algae and fish pee – and the day's wet weather aerating the roots of trees.

Denny walked the maze of red brick and grey stone wishing Kath would call. While they were 'only friends', he could do with her now.

1

'Every day a new chance for the journey, yeah Den'?' Kath would say sometimes when they parted. Friends. Friends! Kath was as good as it got, and he'd only known her a couple of months. He'd had friends when he was a kid but now, where'd the lads go? And, to the point: where were the *girls*? Who ever has enough of them, Denny thought, pitying himself. 'Old Man Nineteen,' his mother told him. Denny only wanted to be 'some*teen*' – and mean something to himself and to the strangers he met every day. And to the others he wouldn't meet except in the dream of a future that he hoped included him.

In Stephen's Green a statue held its head. 'Someone famous once,' Kath pointed out, emphasising *once*. That they'd met up at all was a miracle. That they were friends, best of friends, was some sick fantasy. 'Don't say the sister thing, Denny. I love you like a sister but I'm not your sister, I'm your friend.' But they were more than friends.

Once at the bus station downtown – closer to the ships (as if to make clear: if you're not affording the ship you'll be taking the bus!), he thought he might be in a time-warp between a castle jail and a corridor of sliding doors in a futuristic film. Little mirrors teased him and taunted, set in an army around the columns that held the bottom floor from caving in. It was a cave. Denny was the writing on the wall.

Strangers moved like slices of shadows in the bus station, appearing from the intersection of every right angle multiplied. Stainless lockers stored lighters, hemp bags, notebooks, ear-buds, and electronics that disappeared when the lightness of body recognised shoulders didn't need the weight of constant utility. Denny felt he stuck out. He moved lumbering, as if he took up more space than he should.

And mercy. The lockers stored *mercy*.

Being a pal, Kath suggested they meet outside the gates of the university. Because they weren't students there they felt unduly tentative. Kath waited. Her arms crossed tightly, each hand clutching opposite shoulder blades, her dark blue trenchcoat cut below the knee out of style, her steel-toed brown boots ready to end a fight if ever there was a problem. She held her skeleton like two hands around a pole, or like a mom's around a small kid; or a mate warming a mate.

He was waiting for a text.

Kath was a good friend to have on your side in a confrontation and Denny wanted to remain in Kath's brigade – small enough circle though they were.

2

Imagine Kath, dressed in ripped punk clothing and spikes in her hair, attending their annual Halloween party declaring she was Cuchulain, pins all the way down the seams of her pants and a belt – the size of a prize-fighter's – binding her fit belly. A kick-boxer who busked metal on the side. This is what she looked like, blur of grainy motion-stirred instagram, dagger glare and steam. No one would go near her – and that's what she thought she wanted.

In light rain Denny thought he could be a changeling. The taps on his neck and nose could be the first soft shudders of the warp-spasm he dearly wanted to become – and if not to *become*, to have happen to him. Everyone seemed to be growing up so fast around him, too. Was he really still a kid inside?

My friend, we're all kids forever because once we're kids we can never forget the kids we were.

The distance between being a child and running things on your own is not a big expanse. Denny was new at this. He thought he could be anything: a professional, a good tradesman, even an actor or athlete. Jayz, he might even try to be a politician! This was the time you could simply *decide* what you wanted to do with your life and in a matter of years it would be done.

But wherever Denny went he saw a lot of men and women who appeared old. The old seemed to have stopped part-way, as if, if they had dreams – and you'd be crazy to think they didn't – these dreams had been folded in meat-packing paper and placed in a cigar box in the attic. 'Nobody even sees them,' Denny whispered to himself, shocked by what he was seeing. Ghosts. All of them. A chipmunk climbed a sapling near his shoulder. *Agelessness*, he thought about the striped creature. *The animals of this world are ageless. What a thing: to live forever like this.* One tooth in the chipmunk's mouth over-bit its fur like an outcast or the victim of a crowded mouth. *Poor bastard. He'll never fit in*, Denny decided. Maybe the animals weren't saintly old but they would be replaced, and the living mortals wouldn't know the difference. And maybe we meditate too long, and maybe we never meditate enough. Still, old is old and Denny had a long way to go. He saw a bird exhaust itself taking materials for a nest into a mirrored window. 'It's a wonder anything's alive,' Denny admitted with a blank stare across the canal.

Denny had good eyes.

'Denny, you should take your exams and then become a photographer!' his art teacher told him.

'Then I'd need a camera. Oh, and *money*,' Denny replied.

'You'd *make* money!' the art teacher insisted – although not entirely obvious to both of them. Then she added, 'You have your phone.'

A phone is merely a little computer with big eyes and big ears and apparently you may run the world with it if your name is FleeceBook or McMacNamera or Twilight. *Well I'll just start a band and call myself Silly,* Denny concluded.

A photographer! What a way to be impoverished and ignored, isn't it?

First he had to find where he belonged, *if* he belonged, and to whom he would offer his soul. *Tall order for a Frenchman*, Denny kidded himself. He thought the French were incredibly confident, not to mention good-looking.

Identity wasn't quite a fish in a barrel. You can walk around your whole life and never discover it. You think you've tasted it and you've only ever had crud. At eleven Denny knew he knew what he liked. He was standing at The Bay of Fundy next to a bagpiper, who happened to be a young woman. The rest 'is history'. At sixteen he wished he'd known better. Would it take all his life to be any closer to the music? He started paying attention to people's eyes. Their lips, the way their fingers moved, their eyes, the light behind a person's eyes, the aura around them. But this got him nowhere. He needed to be a saint like his classmate Michael, the lad who would become his first and last university roommate.

*

In Lebanon maybe the bread's better but seven doors from Denny and Michael's flat a Lebanese guy, Al, sold the cheapest loaf Denny knew about in this part of town – thanks first to Michael. With the money he saved Denny could challenge his roomie, and increasingly his up-close-and-personal rival, on the pool table most nights each week. The leisure centre was closer than bread, and next to decent chips too. Denny went there often, although he had a feeling he was no good. Good Michael tried to help, but he tried the way only someone who's really good at something and wants to keep winning will try: a tip's as good as another chance to show off. Michael – Michael Saint Anthony, his given name (and a name to live up to!) – could correct a poorer player's position and be charming and look like an angel while doing it. The young ladies around the table would oogle and caw like they were cooing. But Denny knew, and the lads knew, their Saint Anthony was just showing off. The fact he did it so gracefully was to be admired, especially by Denny – frustrating as it was.

Do you have to be good to be where the action is? Denny was glad he had a friend like Kath so he didn't have to think about how good he was, or wasn't.

Everyone dressed in charity-shop fashion so there was no competing. Denny's favourite hoodie used to be Kath's: Hello Kitty with a tongue out and a grin. Hello Shitty. This in pinks and baby blues. He'd save his Hard Rock one for sleeping.

But here's a secret: if Denny told anyone his parents were from Finglas it was a lie, but that's how he played it after a while. He didn't want to appear like he'd had it easy, like he'd had a mum who pampered him and a dad who worked in an office. Not only was the pampering and the office true, but it was miles – and miles – away. 'Where-y'-from?' Denny hoped he'd never have this question. Michael Saint Anthony never had it, and look how smoothly he fit in. Of course, it was easier for him because the Anthony family had lived in Europe for three years. Michael had developed 'an accent' – one that blended in anywhere. Everyone knew he was from away but for some reason this didn't matter with Saint Anthony. An instantly trusted friend to a stranger, he could get away with being all 'of the people, by the people, for the people'. He was a true bloke.

Can't a bloke set up new rules for himself, avoid the system, have a good time? But Denny's being from Finglas was ridiculous and Denny knew it – which was partly why this was the story and he was slipping through it. For a Yank to say he was from Finglas was like a see-through come-on line in a bar: a bit ironic, because maybe in America people would like the sound of it, not knowing anything about the place. Denny felt he had to be from somewhere, and his friend Kurt, being from Finglas, seemed tall and sturdy – enough of a fine example of a determined young man. Why not be from where a friend is from? This way of thinking gave Denny the chance to 'make it new', as the famous Modernists pounded into anyone who'd pay attention.

Sheet. It was starting to rain. Denny's paper bag started to soil like sand.

Even Kath mocked Denny before they became pals. Then she saw how desperate he must be, how he envied the Saint, and how it must have been for Denny when he was younger and special to his mum and dad. She knew 'desperate'. She recognised in his eyes a soul who felt it was losing. Wasn't it glorious to be nineteen?! Let's double the punctuation on that one, for it is and it isn't. 'Nineteen and counting,' Kath would say. 'Denny, we're not fourteen any longer, we're not *eighteen*. We're *fookin' nine-bloody-teen!* Can you believe it? Where're we going and what're we doing?' Coming from Kath, who could take on an army with her speech and spitfire and sass, this was a little disconcerting to Denny.

Swans slid a white line across the surface of water in Stephen's Green like the girl's hand gliding chalk across the blackboard at Listons. School was for learning, as much about sensual things as numbers and authors' names, their titles, geography, history, sciences. Through every ancient system there was a hand, Denny was sure of it.

The glass of the bus seemed ancient to him. Beads of water serrated across his window like a feathered line at an angle, a sort of interrupted check mark, lifting itself upward. Denny needed to be lifted upward.

His selfie in the landscape through what amounted to a two-way mirror as he journeyed seated, not doing a thing – feeling only a little more sorry for himself than for the working people he saw every day (the bus driver, for instance), this selfie stayed impressed in the bus window until the light changed. It was his stop. He had certain needs and he was determined to walk along the canal and bother Kath for messages.

As he came near Richmond Row he saw a scrum of students bounce out of the institute's steps like cotton balls in blue blazers and shining knees. He'd met a girl at the leisure centre who was a student there. She didn't regularly spend her time in Rathmines, or any mines; 'Usually centre city', she said in reverse – causing Denny to like her even more. She was studying 'Show Business', she said, to which, upon hearing this, Denny laughed – and this was the last time Denny would make this silly mistake. *Never laugh at the girl who's giving you interest. Stay with her story – and only laugh just after she does.* She was a serious young woman and she didn't think Denny was taking her seriously enough – not about who she was or how she looked but about her professional ambitions. She carried a mini tartan-pattern umbrella and had a way of holding it like no other girl, more like an officer, or a signalman whose flare was dynamite but was casual about it. She held it straight down but Denny wanted to see the umbrella go up, to see the softer underside of her arm. She was holding her blue blazer over one arm and stood in her short-sleeved white blouse. *Of course* she'd want to be in show business. How insensitive of Denny to laugh. He would have done anything to see the umbrella open up. He had an idea this would make her smile. She was pretty but he'd forgotten her name.

He was being a boy in reverse. How many young people feel like they inhabit an older person's cloak? He began dwelling on the breakfast he'd had: a thin piece of toast. A little borrowed jam. He'd hoped his flatmates wouldn't notice. He'd only taken a little bit, enough to glom onto the tips of two knives. It was raspberry jam and the deep crimson, almost purple, with amber seeds like little astronauts, reminded him of his grandmother's. Anything *berry* was good with her. His grandfather had gone to milk the single cow the family had. The barn was huge, more grey than brown, and draftier now, nearly a hundred years since it had been built. August hay filled most of the cavern that was the mouth and belly and shoulders of the barn. Down low, on the underside of the slope where the barn was situated, was the muddy entrance to the milking room. Here, a single light bulb hung by a thread of cord two feet from the ceiling, log beams with dust and left-behind years of hay mulched into concise insulation between the cracks. Between the methane, manure, aged wood, corn, hay and animal hide, Denny thought the area smelled like a spicy tobacco.

His grandfather worked the cow in light that seemed so much brighter than one bulb could produce. If he were on stage he'd believe it. A warm pool spread around the milking stool. The aluminum bucket sat in the shadow of the cow's underbelly. The stool, when his grandfather brushed it with the grommet of his sleeve, made a banjo sound. This made the cow dance a little, a shuffling of the hind feet and an affirmation of the front left, as if the animal were digging in – realising it was about time to be relieved. There was something primitive and sensual about all this: the silence and the warmth of bulb, the aroma and the shuffling, the cold circular seat followed by the banjo twang, the full udder looking like a swollen bottom from a fashion magazine and then its striking teats – bloated like a big woman's fingers about to submerge themselves in an apple-pie filling. The animal barely groaned before the first narrow spray hit the base of the aluminum. He met these confusing messages with his adrenalin caught in the dispassionate void of terror and excitement, like a held breath he'd keep while his father cut a board and spread sawdust into the air as the bits of surprisingly soft wood pelted his face like a warmer snow.

In the hierarchy of pain and sadness, Denny didn't think he deserved to feel shoddy. Whatever had happened with the dog, Baby Hey Zeus, or to the cow, one moment being milked and then waiting for the hands that wouldn't reach up again and grab it where it wanted be relieved, or to the car-crash flight of saints who were roommates? He didn't feel he really should be included, and yet he felt the absences, as if their fleeting told him something about himself, about loves, maybe. 'Count on them,' his friend Kurt would tell him. Coming from Kurt, who had nothing except the army, the pool hall, and these few oddball friends, Denny was inclined to hear him – and hear him well.

Minute raindrops freckled Denny's face as he walked away from a raincloud and into the sun. Anyway, he'd rather remember his grandfather in warmer light, like under the bulb. A boy, full steam ahead, would have learned how to milk the cow in seconds, filling the bucket after persistent labor. Instead, he watched – after trying his hand, which looked like it was pulling a rope from a dress, or knocking on a small door for wee people – while his grandfather took over, like an able man rowing a boat.

What was it about this street that reminded Denny of his grandfather? Was it the shadow across the two sides, breakfast toast – barley, maybe, the jam – and the smell of eggs as he passed Camden Street and St Kevin's? And it was the lure of what was ahead, around the certain convictions of St Valentine, who was buried across from the oldest house in the city – the lucky twenty-oner, where a city conceived its fortune in a tongue and a dare. Eventually he'd find a girl who would like him as much as a cow needed to be milked, although he didn't desire to be so pathetic in his daydreams. Then, he wouldn't have to feel like a boy in reverse. His grandfather left the cow beside him, the aroma – cow's breath and the solitary light, as ice hardened on the barn floor beneath him. His heart needed kneading but there was nothing the cow could do. The bulb seemed dim and the stool slid below the cow's hind legs. The bucket of milk stayed intact. It would be a long holiday before Denny would learn to milk a cow.

His body was a sadder shape now, neck and head hunched forward as if he were sending a text, only he wasn't. His nose was above his runners. 'Tits above toes,' he'd heard a coach say when he'd tried cross-country at age fourteen. He found this amusing for several reasons, not the least of which was – point of fact – he didn't have any.

Peter Street was ahead if he kept going down this road. He wondered who Adelaide Chambers was and didn't want to think too much about it or else he'd be thinking, and sure he wanted to, about how Adelaide and Ann Summers were friends. He couldn't stop thinking about it. Oh she must be pretty, Adelaide. And discreet. 'Maybe this is where the "Chambers" came in,' he figured. Even the fact he was figuring anything at all while the name "Adelaide Chambers" was in his mind meant he had a figure in his head, and the word itself: *figure*; this, for a lad without a girlfriend, was both inspiring and awfully sad. *Maybe beneath the surface Adelaide is an Ann?* He had to stop thinking this way or he'd get hit. He liked the idea that Adelaide could be prim and proper, just like the four-storey building that housed cubicles for businesses he didn't want to ever have to understand. He decided he ought to turn. *East, young man! Go east!* he commanded. The west was too alluring. As was this central row.

But what would the girl Ireland look like, really? Would she have long red hair or would she surprise us and look like herself, someone we never dreamed, red or not. *Mimi Holliday? Molly Holiday, Holly Holiday, Holy-holy!*

The cars were so whiny and frequent Denny wished he had one. *Give me a shine; seats of leather.* He'd put it to the streets, gear down into the corners, stop on a coin to meet the light . . . though the idling engine he could afford would sound like a scooter. (He didn't mind; in fact he liked it.) *The girls waiting to cross will see me and say inside themselves, 'Who's the nice-looking guy in the little car that sounds like a kitten purring?'* (More like a puppy coughing, he admitted – but he didn't care; he got a kick out of the idea of it.) It was a little bit of 'show business' that a young man had to put on now and then. Not like the girls. They were at it all the time, it appeared to Denny; ready or not.

How does one study show business anyway? Should she (Cait, her name, Cait, that's it!) move to Hollywood? New York City? Notting Hill? Bollywood? He wondered if sweet Cait and dear Kath would ever have chance to meet. If it were up to Denny they'd be side by side; but this was 'BN': before Nuala.

9

Cait had longer legs than theirs. She took a liking to white, even when others would say it wasn't fashionable. 'As Anglican as a Mediterranean church,' assessed Denny. It was just sheer fate or fortune that Cait happened to be the guest of a friend of a friend that brought her into the arcade. Out of place she was, but she stood there with her friend, either at the side of the video game or at the corner of the pool table, looking like the most radiant beam of hallelujah Denny had ever known. A statue, really. A statue so warm and able to move that someone had offered to put an Arnotts' dapper suit coat over. Even relaxed, she was more regal than anything the leisure centre had seen. There in her royal blue Milly off-the-shoulder flared dress there was no spotlight but anyone could feel her presence if she just moved an inch.

She slipped away into the scrum of Portobello Institute graduates, an increasingly fashionable and self-aware group, and Denny never saw her again. He often wondered if he'd pass her and would she recognise him and pause from conversation with her school friends and let out an enthusiastic 'Denny!' He realised if he wasn't in the same 'Club', if membership was closed, he was on his own.

A toddler stared at him from a simple pram, glaring with wet post-crying cheeks and eyes that seemed to want to transfer the grief.

If there would be no Cait, what would the girl named 'Ireland' be called?

*

Mornings, Denny was the last to leave the white house with the black door – whose number was crooked, as if to throw off anyone who might be calling. It seemed like a house of the destitute.

Moria had lived on the top floor for around thirty years and wasn't even the supervisor. Stephen, who lived in the lowest unit under the stairs, was the supervisor – unlikely as this was, for he couldn't change a bulb and was never home. 'Grumpy Steve,' Kath called him. Steve never gave Kath the time of day.

He never gave anyone the time of day except Simon, his flatmate, and a trannie, Kath surmised. Kath didn't care that Simon was trans, in fact Kath liked a lot of Simon's clothes. She just wished the residents at Denny's address would pay more attention to her friend. He's a likeable guy. Like him!

Plus, don't be a fecken grump?

The Chinese laundry was on the corner on the way to the bus and Denny and Kath both liked to inhale the 'hotel-clean' aroma oozing out of the cracks and imagine themselves in the fine starched sheets of The Clarence. Before the traffic light they'd hug, pretending to be a couple leaving The Clarence for dinner with posh guests, waving off the paparazzi.

Neither of them had used the Chinese laundry. They made a pact: one day, 'when we're famous', they'd stay in such a place – famous or not.

A school allowance kept Denny just above desperate and if he kept inheriting Kath's clothes he'd be fine. Hello Shitty could stay around a lifetime.

Chapter Two

When he wasn't with Kath he was alone or following Saint Anthony. Michael Saint Anthony, simply 'the Saint', as Denny and Kath were quick to call him behind his back, was what they'd called in the States a 'Golden Boy'. If he smiled – a wide grinny one that easily slipped into place on command – he'd get the girl. If he turned around while standing in place, no matter where he was, he could get a job on a hand-shake with a stranger. Anthony had a glint to his eyes – which only made him more 'saintly'. Tall, good looking, the Saint was goofy too, but no one ever seemed to see his goofiness. To everyone else he was suave, a greased machine, a can-do-no-wrong Yank-of-all-trades guy.

There was one exception to the rule of three (being with Kath, alone, or with the Saint), and this was being with Kurt. Kurt the magician! One week he worked as a mechanic, the next he was going to be a priest, and then he was a soldier boy. The leisure centre attracted a mixed crowd and Kurt was one of the constants among them. He was 'Sarge', as Kath was the first to call him. Denny would have liked to call him 'Kurt' just as well, but 'Sarge' worked for him also. *Sarge*. There was something commanding about Kurt, but not in a golden way like the Saint's. Kurt, as 'Sarge', was dirty brass people like Kath wanted to shine. Kitten Kurt. Someone would want to pick him up and comb him proper – if he'd let them.

He was a little older, and older guys like Kurt had it under control – or at least they made it look this way. Kurt was never easily flustered but Denny understood Kurt was, at one time, on the edge – and could be again, if things didn't go his way. Kurt would walk instead of take the

12

bus and Denny figured it was to save money. Kath said it had something to do with his family. It wasn't thriftiness. Kurt never had much 'quid' (as was the expression Kurt himself continued to use, like an old man) – even though, among his friends, he held the only real honest jobs in those first months when they were all getting to know each other.

Denny envied how the Saint and Sarge got along. Both lanky and amiable, they were both aces at pool and snooker – which helped them become friends of the lads and admired, due to the attention they received from the lads – and the ladies. And each seemed upon first impression quiet, reserved – even though these are the ones who are the most cunning and devilish, sometimes. Like gold and brass. But Sarge's smile was different. It was more like a frown, as if he was always either mad or thinking about something really important. And yet girls went for him. 'Do you like music?' one would ask. 'Yeah. Sure I do. I like you,' Sarge would say. And that was that. Usually she'd write her phone number or transfer it then and there, whipping out her glittery sticker-covered phone – the size of a handheld mirror that fit snug in her palm like it was used to it.

No worries. The whole enchilada. Spoonfuls of honey. Match maker match maker . . .

Michael Saint Anthony didn't wait for the phone, though. He was usually already leaned over and kissing the girl before anyone said anything about numbers. Girls liked how lean he was. 'Smooth like a razor clam.' 'Intoxicating,' said one, despite the fact she'd only ever seen him from the far corner of the leisure centre. It must have been like seeing a buck in the field to her; the hens reacted viscerally to the sight of Saint Anthony.

Denny tended to get the parents, once the number was finally passed along through the young lady's friends. 'This is Sheila's dad. I've got her phone for a while. Don't call back – while you're alive!'

Startled, this was how Denny never got a date – though he blamed it on his pool game.

Still he tried. Ponytail ponytail, rig-a-jig-jig. The shore's liquid, sniffed by a pig.

The shudder of silence from the girl's father and from the girls he wanted to meet affected Denny (who hadn't thought he'd done anything wrong) in the typical ways: he'd retreat further into himself, play computer games, listen to music, and watch the fun other people were having with feigned detachment, disdain and a tried-true pitiful self-acknowledged melancholy that could either be an adorable code for 'talk to me, I've got nothing to lose' or a force-field stench – like the ever-hopeful Linus in Peanuts, though Denny certainly thought of himself more like Charlie Brown. Kath can keep her role in the mongrel cast of any Moloney's loosey-toon comics, Denny fumed. She'd always have a supporting part.

Some girls have all the luck. Period. Gotcha. Spread a rose on polka dots for smiles.

'For fuck's sake,' Kath would tell him, 'don't just stand there and take it' – even though she was jealous because of what she saw as possible for Denny. What she really meant was that he shouldn't compare himself to the Saint or Sarge. He was his own man. Barely out of his teens, he had his own gifts and Kath was going to help him find them. She wasn't sure whether it would be as a friend or as a good-good friend. It could go either way, and frankly, this pleased both of them.

'You know, the great Johnny Logan never faltered on his road to Eurovision,' Kath said as a challenge.

'*Right.*' Denny bit back, 'Oh, *Hold Me Now* . . . . And a Nik Kershaw to your Howard Jones while you're at it!'

Kath smiled. A Luas-across-a-bridge kind of smile. She knew she'd be late with it but it was there.

Spring's gorge in the pocket of George Washington. Simon Says in the charity shop. Easy does it!

They were getting on.

At Dalkey he sat by the water where the sun made a warm tide-mark across his knees. Kath played ukulele and sang Seattle grunge songs in the smoky alto of a female Cuchulain, sounding more like Chloë March than a doomslayer. Even so, 'I could do with a little less grunge and a lot more Phoenix, Kath!' Denny critiqued, only half-earnestly playing the buzz-kill.

'You'd do anything for the French! It's amazing you're still in Ireland,' Kath said – probably teasingly insinuating the lack of any kissing Denny was doing in Ireland.

But there they were, more armchair mariners than grounded nationalists. The sun felt like two hands of a professional, a professional anything, and they were happy to obey the invitation to be leisurely together. They laughed at their unemployability and bumped shoulders seated on the ground next to one another. The goats were probably making a fuss on the little island, on the other side of the tower where Denny first met Kath. They were friends for less than a year but they may as well have been mates for life. The whole scene, and the scenes of everyday, actually, were ridiculously funny when Denny and Kath were together. Why couldn't the hours be so easy when Denny was with the Saint or Sarge? Guys grow silent in the woods. They were rough saws together, Kath and Denny, different types of rocks, but their friendship was solid, as if by command, and as if they were related but not from the same mother.

Handkerchief, snot-rag, booie-blocker, turtle sand. They shared their messages like glue.

Friends are like doorknobs, Denny decided. Some feel good but they're greasy. You never know where they've been, what came before, how soon they're going to turn. Some look polished but inside they're frantic and falling apart. The ragged ones are sometimes the best. Inside, you've got nothing to lose.

He didn't think the Saint or Sarge ever had anything to lose, but for different reasons. The Saint had it from the beginning. Sarge was a work in progress, but one for whom life's compensations matched the struggle.

If they'd been a band their individuality would be understandable. Not being a band, they were an odd ensemble: Boy Scouts who had lost their troop. But according to the schedule of their lives they were naturally previously unknown to each other – and this was both scary and hopeful, like entering a new school. On one hand, it was scary if it meant Denny would always be meeting strangers who would count as friends, but never again a friend who was a friend before. He wished he'd known Kath before. It was, on the other hand, hopeful because in a way it meant he'd never have to grow old. He'd be a mirror to his friends, but his friends would always be new. Or so he told himself. What did the schedule of their lives have to do with anything anyway? They weren't planning on playing by anyone else's time. Each day was their day. Denny just had to beef up, man up, and let Kath whisper what mattered in his ear.

The exception to Denny's theory about only ever meeting new friends, strangers who were somehow loners like him, was with the Saint, for indeed Denny and Michael Saint Anthony had had a history together, back home. To have known somebody in their hometown and to have to know them on another level outside of the past, to have visited each other's families while they were innocent of perspective beyond the fields of play, merely fulfilling the recreational alliance of kids who are neighbors, not only to have been in primary school together but to study in the same university classes, to have watched each other grow up and then be assigned the same room in a dorm and then in a flat far from anything they knew to be familiar in the sense of 'home'; this was a friendship that stayed strange, for they were close enough to have a feeling about each other's thoughts. Brothers without a shared heritage. Until Dublin, they looked out for each other unconsciously.

Chapter Three

'It's a bridge and a cliff to sunrise' was all Denny could say to Kath as they watched Dalkey pass by from the train. He was feeling at home but he was still the outsider trying to fit in.

'Maybe you need new clothes,' Kath said, to be helpful. It was true, he had a limited wardrobe: five jeans, his father's hand-me-down Marine coat, some plaid flannel shirts, eight or nine T-shirts, only a few socks and underwear, a baseball cap from a team he no longer followed, and a rain slicker, runners, pointy shoes he bought in Belfast, and banged-up hiking boots he rescued from a charity-shop window.

He was Irish and he wasn't. He felt he had ambition but it was a tough show. Who'd believe the kid in the Shitty hoodie? 'Ambition's for sissies,' Sarge told Denny from across the pool table two seconds before Sarge sunk the eightball in the side pocket from way down the green, a hard shot to amateurs like Den'. Denny wasn't sure whether Sarge was kidding or not – which was occasionally a problem with Sarge. And then he heard Kath's voice, too warm and too wet in his ear, like she was getting the wrong idea, hanging around the Sheilas and Lassies of leisure too much. But always comforting, she stated familiar ideas as though they were worn flannels, like pyjamas, like just shy of a whole foot-rub: 'Remember, Den', *there'll be days like this.*' She was quoting a song they both sang when they were overlooking the goats and the Irish Sea north of Bray, the town Denny had intended to visit but never got to explore when they'd spent the day together along the coast south of Dublin, when the sun branded their knees.

17

They'd been locked-in during their mutual acquaintance with Dalkey Island because the goats and tides held them in no man's land, as if the gods decided they should be friends. 'The "gods",' they both wondered, seventy percent condescendingly.

Do the gods have ambition? (And whose gods are these, again?) Denny prayed to the gods of turf and sky, peat and daydreams in the smoky swirls of the inner eyes; 'to meat and moss, weave and skin','as he told Sarge in a moment of reverie. And to youthful sins that in time and love are never really *civic* sins or crimes against the population or nature. In fact, these are acts of and *for* the population, by and to nature, to the goodness of what every man and woman finds there within a lifetime. Maybe the gods of photography, poetry, fashion, relented for the sanity of sentient beings in this situation. Or maybe moss just hugs a stone and meat wraps all its fibres around the blood and bone of what will breathe and be found.

Kath and Denny had returned to the scene of the tides for old times' sake, only a few months after they became friends. The bridges and cliffs would be several and many in their lifetime but they had a feeling they'd be encountering many of them together.

A lad is a dreamy oak in a cloud blanket. A lass is a lad with double *s*'s. Anything in between is cherry pie. And Grafton Street stays lit all night.

*

It rained like this in Barrentown and it rained like this in Greads. Denny thought at least on the coast the rain was greeted in kind, wet on wet. Like a lad looking in the mirror at six, nine, sixteen, twenty-two, twenty-seven, thirty-four, forty, sixty . . . One wave rolled into the other and slant of rain became slant of wave. 'It should be *sláinte*,' he said inside himself, emphasising the 'i' and the 'e' as if a body could appendage a new soul. He meant, 'What's good in the mirror is good in the self.' Denny wasn't sure that would stand so true for the girls. Since he wasn't a girl he couldn't know, but he figured. He suspected sometimes mirrors hide what's good within. So why wouldn't every rainfall be good for the body – and good for the soul? How fertile the rain, though; how insistent. He could tell his sense of self was rubbing up against ambition. If finding a reason is ambition then Sarge was wrong, or else Sarge was kidding. 'Eightball, side pocket!' It seemed sure as ambition. 'Corner girl in my eye's socket!' Denny tried to parody to himself. For his roommate it would be 'the cover girl', and without trying.

He felt the rain tapping the shoulders of his father's military jacket and saw, in his mind's wildest eye, a row of three step-dancers hopping up and down as if on sticky tape, like they were costumed mice in a glue-trap lit by a stage. They were cuter than your average three mice but their white breasts looked like shorn fur crests that should have sent a message about ambition. Soon they would be whitecaps, or snowflakes in Wicklow.

It was too easy to forget that in Dublin – with a good many parks and all that vertical green, as in Merrion Square's little lost forests Denny grew to love like the fantasy side of a looking glass – the machinery around him, automobiles, buses, lorries, brick and mortar, made it ridiculously easy to forget that the city sat on the edge of a sea, and you'd never know it from Rathmines. Sweet dry brine wafted through the automobile air, probably Silverskin's from Ballsbridge. The thought of it made him laugh out loud. Kath would appreciate all the LOLs bursting in Denny's head. Jayzus, it didn't take much: Silverskin, Ballsbridge. He had to wonder, was it this particular city, Dublin, or was it his age? Both, maybe. But likely throughout the world the Silverskins and Ballsbridges, the coffee-bean aroma melding with whatever was near – sea brine or wheat, the kid in their parent's army coat or the girl with the furry chest straight out of the school's costume trunk, the lad in Stokestown shorts on the wrong side of friendly divides; Denny felt sure that somewhere – somewhere times plenty – the Kaths and Dennys of the universe were dreaming in the rain of warmer things, and excitement was sure to be lit in the eyes of a stranger they were bound to meet – simply because they had kept their eyes watching for an otherwise unseen bay of stars. Something good depends.

The coffee roast was pungent – as it hadn't been in a while – almost methane, and for a few seconds Denny was feeling again what it was to be soaked on the road out west. Either a lift or a ride would have been nice, right about then. And camp coffee, rebellion brew, for the turf-keepers. *Come on, boys, pick me up. Someone: pick me up.* Of course it could have been Mr Hobbs. Silverskin and Hobbs shared some common grounds, you could say, when it came to beans in the sack. 'How many T-shirts can fit in the Ballsbridge kiosk?' goes the joke. 'Dunno.

How many T-shirts fit in the Ballsbridge kiosk?' a person's supposed to ask. 'Well, you fit Ms Dublin, Ms North, Ms Ooh-La-La and Ms Galway all the way – except you'd be asking for more than "tay" at the Ballsbridge kiosk!' It was only a little funny the way Sarge told it but it was funnier to Denny as he recounted it, smelling the singed stuff like the gone days of waistcoats around the red-light district. *Some men's beans have all the luck*, lamented Denny. He was talking to himself as much as to please Sarge. He might have been saying as much to the men of the turf, to Mr Hobbs and Silverskin, to his own two – bollocks. Out west, the number of rigs and motorcars that passed him up equalled the Ms Dublins, Norths, Ooh-La-Las, Galways that did the same. 'All-ways Galways,' Sarge insisted. Sexist bastard or fool. They didn't know what they were saying, half the time! One thing for sure: there was certainly no all-ways in Galway for Denny. Galway had changed with the Tiger. The Lion and the Lamb were over. But maybe things would get back again and Denny would find himself in one of those second homes overlooking the trad stuff, snuggling the Lamb. But hadn't the tiger eaten the Lion and the Lamb? Or else the Lion had gone into hiding with the Lamb. Ballsbridge to stonewalls, Denny thought he could be the guy the Tiger and the Lion and the Lamb sought. And couldn't he also be a saint? 'Saint Denny': it had a ring to it, but it also felt false to Denny. He hadn't quite earned it. Good? Yes, he was good. But no one saw him as a saint.

Kath had claimed he looked 'blue as *that clock*!' when they heard the double strike at Trinity's gates. 'Three-legged gravity. What'd you expect?' said Denny. She knew what he was referring to; she'd been around the block all right, but if she'd been his sister he would have told her a lot sooner. As it was, Kath liked Denny and so he tried to limit his blunders to only once in a while. In reality, Kath let 'em go just as often – encouraging no limits between friends. Nevertheless she could tease like an iron skillet. 'Um, you and your tree-legged grav't' can be wound 'as infrequently as possible' if you keep up that rot, Mis-stir Denny!' – quoting the manual, giving her patent blast as much feminista authority as she could rollick on the spot. The truth was, they both liked the man and the woman of it, Wordsworth's dong and ding, like an echo of the unsilent other, as a reminder that maybe Ms North and Mr South did have a place on the same keychain, as it were.

After all, Mr Hobbs had a market advantage with the fortunate help of Mrs Hobbs. Stormtroopers, cyclists, race-car drivers, beauty queens and Mrs Hobbs. 'No wonder he drove a red truck!' Denny said. 'That's an inside joke,' Kath completed with hardly a gap, a sleek reference to 'Little Red Corvette'. They both liked Prince. But there was no red; there'd be no purple.

Still: blue. Blue Kona, blue beans, blue on blue. The things looked for, how quickly they disappeared. Except, maybe, blues.

He came around from daydreaming to where he thought he would: away from the sea and into the middle of Dublin – at least the middle to him – feeling hungry. Listons Fine Food and Pastries became a symbol of everything Denny wanted but couldn't afford on a daily basis, not as long as he remained in the 'between student and what' purgatory – like ninety percent of all the other students. 'But the rest of them have home and I'm a traveller,' Denny said pityingly.

Through the steamed window he saw the sway of the barista's white apron at the hip. The rest was foggy. He could hear the clatter of the plates and utensils muted through the glass and, better, as the door opened he could smell coffee and muffins, and hear the warm laughter of a patron and one of the girls at the counter as they said goodbye. The rain was more like a spray in the day's moderate temperature and Denny felt himself 'very coastal' – as his teacher used to say about anyone who wore a cable-knit sweater to class, and not as a compliment. If it took being a sailor to be hungry enough to go to town and open a door, he supposed he could be this sailor now.

Once inside, Denny thought he'd come home. He wanted to linger and felt the welcome of this waiting room like the day he was a kid, one Halloween, when he'd seen for the first time his neighbour's stately front room with all its bronze-tinged wallpaper and deep-sea trophies intriguing him as if there was something sociological beneath it. 'Maybe she'll see me through the chalk. Maybe her hand needs a wet rag.' He was by now watching the hand that was undoubtedly connected to the caramel-coloured ponytail, the way she made waves in cursive along the chalkboard as she copied the daily menu. Denny kept thinking about things that amused him because of their inconsequence. But he knew something about objects, by now, that represented the states of people – like Prince and his Corvette. 'Her wet rag which is my rain-soaked shirt,' Denny made clear to himself, as if to seal the fiction that said the two of them could be related.

'Perhaps I'll tell her I'm driftwood. Ask her to sit for a while. *Ask* her to sit with me for a while. Through the chalk of her handwriting, I know I know her swirls and think I understand her fancy, *Like* her site, on sight; and all that! And would she like mine? Would she like to sit for a hard-earned break on driftwood? Any girl who writes with chalk like she does would like driftwood too.'

Who even dreams like that? He wanted to imagine what it would be like to be face to face, chest to chest, with the person whose hand it was. He felt her hand and it was alive. Not moist but humid. The skin was warm – like a face in the window where there was sunlight. Her eyes and mouth were partly her hands. When he felt her hand he could see her eyes more clearly, the hundreds of rays that spoke out of the centre, the language that she would want to use, the sound and temperature of her tongue.

Denny looked around at the other customers and wished Kath were with him. 'The only thing wooden about you, mister, is that you don't get the drift – you're missing your stars; you're counting your blue-blue graveyards before you ever hold a slipper in your left hand and a warm foot in your right,' she'd say to him to goad him into a proper reality. 'Denny the Dreamer, you are – but below ground!' 'For fuck's sake, Denny, ask the girl out if you're gonna, or order a muffin and be gone if you're not!' What a good conscience, that Kath. Like a parrot! But the thought of a muffin, a banana muffin with blueberries and nuts – especially if it were warm, steamy when opened, a slab of KerryGold melting 'tween its innards – was as unsettling as thinking about the girl's hand smoothing flaky waves and sewing bows over the chalkboard with every crossed 't' and the bound bottoms of each 'y'. *The old 'y' knot*, Denny guessed. He didn't know what had got him started. He'd blame it on what stirred after the school bell around Portobello, at the edges of Peter Street – Ballsbridge notwithstanding – outside the black door of 128 Lower Rathmines Road.

But for a guy who could experience all this flutter in front of the glass case at Listons, he could feel the insensitivity too – and he wanted to break it. Every kid who ever lived had done a stupid thing but Denny hoped he must be an exception. This didn't last long without money to spend beyond Rathmines. He remembered Shawna, singing to old Sinead O'Connor songs on the hillside outside the school lounge, and how he and Michael had recorded her and posted it on every social-media place they could think of. They hated themselves, later. '*Stretched On Your Grave* is a fuckin' tough song, Michael!' Denny said as soon as he started to feel guilty. (He realised what a lousy thing it was the next time he saw her.) Shawna was a sweetie, a flatmate sister, and Michael and Denny both liked Shawna.

Have you ever heard yourself singing – I mean just to the air, with buds in your ears?

She had been a bird without a song, Shawna, and what Michael and Denny did was mean. There were plenty of *Likes* and only a few close friends of hers to thumbs-down their unthinkable meanness. Sure, it didn't help that Michael and Denny routinely made fun of the girl singer with the shaved head and a mouth and instincts like a bloke. Truth was, they both really liked the shaved head, the instincts, the mouth. They wanted to be more like Sinead O'Connor. Boy versions of Sinead O'Connor. Who cares what Lorne Michaels thinks!

They'd nearly lost a sister. Boys to Men, capital 'M', they were not. They were somewhere in between.

Maybe the universe should be more like gardens and beaches with girls singing – singing from their buds. Kath told Denny about one time in Spain when she was an exchange student. The family had a raft the size of two people where they lived along a river: 'Joni's River', she called it. Two boulders like hearts rested at opposite ends in the section of river you could see from the house where Kath spent three weeks. Homesick, she would go out and ride a slow and easy swirl of current that came around on itself where the river had created a natural pool above a series of short falls. In the unseasonably warm days before it was time to leave and return to school back home, homesick no more, Kath would drift – imagining she were the arm of a clock that played with time, rewinding it and starting over. Her body, curled a little, looked like the lips of a smile on the peach raft with the river's two boulders for her eyes.

They hadn't yet learned flirting. Teasing still felt like the thing they wanted to do, maybe because it enabled them to stick with their friends longer. They didn't have to choose between male and female, the leisure centre or the cinema. Growing up this way, you could still be a kid.

But if it wasn't Kath giving him guidance, it was Sarge or Mick giving him a hard time. It was still a long way to Bushy Park but from the old flat at Rathmines it wasn't so far outside the imagination. Sarge was always sure to point this out.

Denny wanted to fling his red rag at Sarge but it was all brotherly craic. He carried the red rag in the loop of his pants. From far away this looked like a holster. For Denny to look like a cowboy was somewhat appropriate and the idea amused Sarge. The shopkeeper down the block and across the street at Blackberry Lane had a box of these red-red rags, and that day Denny was a ragtag empty sack of his student self, half admiring the rusted cars outside waiting for repair, and half delirious as to why he'd stepped inside the garage; he took to striking up a conversation with the shop owner, Gordon Mernough. Mernough wore a French mechanic's cap and was somewhere between the wheel-well and the drive-shaft when he didn't so much invite Denny in as didn't tell him to leave.

From then on Denny was growing his first soft beard, a rite of passage, the sprigs of which he finally pushed out and tried to adopt, with the help of pharmacies Hickey and McCabe's. His friends had tried piercings and tattoos. It took Denny one time and forever to breed even the sparest clump of stubble. Not surprisingly, it came in no rush. *May the end of me be slow, and fulfilling also*, he'd accepted. *Just like* . . . He couldn't finish his *Just like* . . . because he'd barely gotten here. He was still admiring the arm-skin of the few girls who'd wind up in the leisure centre after school. But by using this measure of 'geologic time', as Sarge taunted, he was still getting used to tying his own shoes! 'They're young *women*, Denny, not "girls",' Kath, the educator, tried to imprint on him. Really it was Sarge and Michael and Mick she should probably have been worrying about. It was every guy, and it was the *boys* who'd become men, strangers and friends. 'We should try to keep ourselves as young as we can,' said Sarge somewhat excitedly – which was out of character. *Easy for him to say*, thought Kath. *Sarge is always a boy*. And there's the double standard – not to mention Sarge seemed to be a man, it would be hard to argue (mature or not, that was another story). Soldier boy, if nothing else other than gaming and holding down a job – if you consider what goes on at the barracks to be gainful, and employment – well, he was meeting the low bar for adult-like qualities.

Across the pool table Denny balled up the rag and pretended to throw it at Sarge. Then he looked down to his side and tied it loosely around the belt-loop at his hip.

'Have you been to Bushy Park yet, Denny?' Sarge would ask in front of half a dozen mates around the table as Denny leaned over and positioned the cue-stick between the soft part of his thumb and the fleshy rise of forefinger. 'It's a ways south, you know, Denny. You know? South of where you've probably never been?'

The lads laughed. Kath, thankfully, wasn't there this time. Denny took people to be kind and didn't always catch on that someone might be kidding until it was too late. *Fine, let me be the object of your jokes,* Denny had to say to himself. *He who laughs . . .*

Denny left the lads at the pool table and left the suddenly insipid pop music too, which he usually liked, blaring on the walls as if to hypnotise him into gummy passion – but for what, he hadn't acquired the tools. To step outside was to put the muffle of a heavy coat over his head, for the decibels of the leisure centre practically totally vanished on Lower Rathmines. He saw the ordinary people, grown-up people, carrying grocery bags, pushing prams, talking quietly on their phones, and he recognised nobody and no one looked toward him. There, where the entertainment met the street, was a vast gap, and quiet too. He walked south toward Rathgar, where he normally didn't think to go. Around the corner there was an orange and green poster for a band: The Goods, they called themselves. It said they'd be featured that night, and they were playing inside the window. The lead singer, a woman wearing a sheath of silver spangles, bobbed her asymmetrical Spanish haircut from side to side. Denny couldn't hear what she was singing but he thought he could like her music anyway. Time after time, Sarge said to Denny, 'it's about time you go a little crazy before that heart of yours stops.' He felt his heart had stopped. He kept up a good front: 'Unless crazy ends-me-up like a plaster Cupid forever wanting my next move on the ceiling of Casino Marino,' Denny rattled back at him, using the best 'Sarge' imitation he could produce. 'I'd rather be *good* than be caught sideways going to hell!' The point of each was that they could be both. No one was saying a person had to be all good and no one was saying there wasn't a little good in crazy. Sarge was looking out for Denny and Denny knew this. Now Denny hoped Denny would find the right manhood and attract the easy friends for Denny's sake. He was a small machine that had never been touched. 'Yes, sir, and four good tires!' Kath would say, kicking his shoes.

He kept walking south and liked the feeling of making his own way, away from the city. *I'll walk to Cork if I have to*, he told himself, pitifully. In fact, as far south as Birmingham (Alabam') there was a place Denny had been and wanted to frequent. He just hadn't taken the low roads all the way. No one noticed him as a willing traveller then, he guessed. Kath was his best bet but what he shared with Kath was something so different, like the robin and the magpie shaking the same tree.

Chapter Four

They didn't know what they were to each other. Those days in Rathmines weren't confusing, exactly, they were just fleeting due to everyone being so busy and, alternatively, *vacant*, like the space for a life that's supposed to look ahead – and know something for sure, or at least almost for sure: plan a future, be ambitious or stunning or darling, have a couple of million followers. No one ever tells you when you're some-teen, twenty-something, whatever the age: those dreams are never perfect. Someone always suffers a breakup, unforeseen, or dies before they or anyone around them is ready.

The clouds move over the spires and tanks and towers of the city at the speed of breath in pipes making music in 'Raglan Road'. A magpie pulls a corpse with all its insistent but begging strength. From above, this looks like a praying nun, only she's tugging on the white washcloth over a foot that represents the world. Her hands, you can't tell, knead the tips of the toes, length of every bone, the fleshy ball and hollow area to the side and centre that sends electricity, and over and around the heel, from the dead to the living. The shadow from the clouds imitates her, or the magpie, and the corpse – sheathed – continues to cross the city. Somewhere delightful, Anna Summers' several stone of fat and blood, musk and muscle, push the lightness of stockings through air to the side of O'Connell, and the recumbent and mild are no longer meek but observant, and taking no prisoners within their own will, or bodies. 'How do we get from there to here?' Kath asked Den', as if the point were always to grab what's popular and inhabit it. But Kath was being ironic also. Maybe, like each of us, she wanted it too. Like we all do, for a moment she thought she could use it. It's tempting – to be tempted. It's as if the brand coaxes a sense of freedom inside us, but really it co-opts a secure feeling we feel we want when we make the purchase.

A shiny shoe, stocking, perfume; a shiny coin on the curb's rim. Curve of a bumper, bannister, tree-knot. Heaven forbid it. Say hail and it hits you in the eye!

Kath and Denny rounded the corner at Kilmainham Jail, before the row of single-window houses, low along the street like the houses were ashamed – but now they were peeking out, asking for forgiveness. Kath thought they were sweet.

'Let's live in one of those, Den'!' She was flirting a little.

Denny was surprised. To flirt so close to a jail? Was this some sort of fecked-up omen? Was he destined to go nowhere before the age of . . .

He couldn't finish the thought. Instead he concentrated on what Kath had said.

The row-houses seemed like kids waiting in the queue, or staring sleepy-eyed at the teacher. The first in line was the saddest because he always wanted to be the first in line – and since he was always the first in line, he was always disappointed. Too often he wasn't noticed. The leaps and bounds he calculated to place his bags at the head of queue, the actual placing of the backpack – like scoring the first and then the winning goal in every game he played, who saw these?

'Think you'd want to know who lived there, Den'?'

Denny realised these were the quarters for workers who once served the jail.

'Now you would – I'm not saying you wouldn't. Good people take over bad places. The places themselves aren't bad – they had nothin' to do with it.' Kath was correct. Good people are everywhere and some of them make a bad place better.

'We could invite Sarge, and he'd feel right at home,' Kath said, laughing.

A home next to a prison is like a room in a barracks, Denny summarised in his mind.

The curve in the road was ominous but the neighborhood seemed to forgive what stood next to it. The wall was more geologic, a base for what would grow here centuries later.

Kath said, 'You know, plenty of people have made out next to that wall, so don't feel so bleeding sad.'

Making out? It had been a good while since anyone had made out with Denny. The fact that Kath was being such a flirt – and she was only a friend – made him feel things were possible again, that maybe someone liked him well enough to love him – even only once.

The school around the bend was new and looked like a ship. Long wooden planks buckled the sleek concrete and glass, and the structure bowed in the centre, making points of its two ends. Anyone would be ready for a journey there, Denny thought. He wished he'd gone to school at a place like it.

In fact he had. When he was twelve. A new school: wood planks, concrete and glass. Maybe this is why he noticed the school near Kilmainham. His had no points, though. Boxcar, shipping container, 'casket', he even fathomed. He would like to have gone to a school with points, set at an interesting angle, as the national school was, instead of the straight-on billboard that his had been.

Kath was a good student but not all of the teachers liked her. Whether quiet or funny, one thing upon which her teachers agreed was that she was smart, usually respectful, and had a gift of perception that was rare among students.

'Oh, forget the jail and let's just move in! I'll paint the outside pink and you can paint the inside blue.'

'Sounds like a song,' Denny said. And then Kath started to sing.

'Joni Mitchell?' Denny guessed. His hippie parents played her stuff a lot (that and Johnny Cash).

'Pure Kath,' Kath underscored.

It was time to go for an ice cream, and Annie's had just opened. 'Breakfast of champions,' Denny rationalised. 'Breakfast for chimps!' Kath mocked.

It was the 'Order of the Disorder' when they were together.

Chimps are champs too – at least at the zoo.

*

Out west, Denny pursued the comedy of a playboy. He'd walked Synge Street enough in Dublin and he thought he ought to give 'being a playboy' a try. Maybe Kath was right and he needed to man up – which sounded awfully antifeminist, come to think of it – and cut the shallow Yank of who he really was on the rugged rock where time doesn't matter.

He felt the way he did when four large bills had dropped from his pocket on the lawn tractor when he was mowing his father's field and saw the portraits and the digits in shredded bits, confetti chewed and coughed out laughably by the mower-blades. 'Cricket food – and not the sport.' 'A waste.' He'd never be good at saving money – but at least it wasn't his phone. Sarge had made that mistake, swimming in the river the night they'd all been to see U2 in Phoenix Park. For months after the others teased him with the refrain (a funny word to use in this case since they did anything but): 'You still haven't found what you were looking for, have you Sarge?' Apart from the phone lost in the river, it was Denny doing all the looking (for each of them, he felt); although, it's true, he didn't know what the others were looking for inside their own skin. Sometimes he had a hunch. But other times he just felt like he'd never have a hunch again. One year they're with you, another year they're gone. A lad like Denny could grow sick thinking about it too much.

This time there was no Sarge and the music was in Denny's head. The Saint was off on one of his adventures – not far away actually, but far in every other way. He'd been invited to a place he refused to discuss upon his return, but from all Denny gathered it was a remote and most privileged retreat about half an hour from Salthill. Denny had been near the place, once, only there was nothing special about the time – it was a haze spent under the spell of his friend Mick's desire in the basement European dance club where the wrong drinks were all the fashion and the young woman only looked over his head and to the sides of his shoulders. Denny thought maybe he smelled of body odour – but it was only the lingering smell of travel, maybe musty blankets and baking soda for clothing detergent. 'A bit more gamey than "meat and moss".' Or maybe it was just how Denny smelled to others. Maybe the girls could smell the lower-rank suburbs that were, in fact, his true home. All this pretending: was it pretending or desire? Do you grow up or do you only grow into where you're from? He tried to dance with the two young women from Germany and the princess from Iceland but they hovered around Mick practically as though he were a pole. Denny faced a panel of lights and danced deep into the light they cast, imagining himself a star the others could not see in the blaze of mirrors. He forced a bliss that was as much synthetic hallucination as reverie – and there he danced in a small square that became his only truth.

Morning came as part of night. Nothing like sleep could exist and Denny felt he'd missed a day, been cheated in order to go to the club with Mick.

'Meet you in San Louis,' Denny said to Mick, kind of mocking, flatly. They were to reunite at one of the three pubs in Doolin. They didn't know where they were going to stay but Mick had a tarp and a rope and he was known to make a tent anywhere – including inside a hostel dining room if he couldn't afford accommodation. To Denny, Mic was the Indiana Jones of international travel. 'A real "IHOP" there, mister . . . ' Denny wanted to say as they parted, referring as much to the sap product at the international house of breakfasts as to the waitresses in flounce.

Denny left first while Mick stayed behind to mix up the make-up of the girl from Iceland, Apples to Apples. The two Germans had their own party starting. Denny could almost hear the suction sound it would take to get Mick to pry himself apart from all this international lovemaking. 'More games, lads! This is all the world needs: more games!' Mick would say, as if he alone were the harmony ambassador of the universe.

Denny's own heart was a sack of air, ziplocked and fluttering, within an all-but-empty mildewed hope-chest his grandfather had brought down from the attic. *Fine, get on with it*, Den' told himself. *If this is what it's going to be like, I should get used to it, right?* Just then, he heard Kath's voice although it was clear she wasn't there.

'Fook yrself!' she exclaimed, making the words sound like 'Look at yourself!' – the way she would say it to him along the canal or in the city centre – anywhere where Denny might be making an ass of himself, wallowing for Kath until she'd kick him in the pants.

He started hitchhiking, something he didn't usually do alone, and after about the sixteenth car he got a lift from what seemed like a jovial crew. The fun lasted only a fraction of that first minute when Denny, now in one of the rear seats, was aware the trio had been imbibing – probably stopping at every watering hole along their way (a way to which they were oblivious). What appeared to be good fun turned aggressive, although the three continued to use the facade of laughter.

'Nice cap,' the driver mocked, for he laughed when he purposely mis-pronounced it, not needing to fake his own drunkenness but he did anyway, saying 'nice crap' – pointing in the rearview mirror his head.

Denny wanted to remark that the man had indeed pointed to his own head. He knew he was being belittled. The night before, and all his adolescent life, had prepared him for more of it.

'Yes, it's a nice cap,' the lady in the passenger's seat soothed even as she seethed with ridicule. They all laughed. It was Kerry tweed, a patchwork of others – not yet popular among the tourists, and it probably would never be popular with the locals unless they became suddenly preppy throughout the land. It could happen. Denny identified with the hodgepodge pattern the first time he saw one in Harrold's on Dame Street. 'F'k yeah. I'm a little of this, a little of that,' Kath had told Denny, describing herself, and Den' had liked this about Kath. Kath bought the woolly wedge for Denny, even if it suited her better, saying, 'One day, Mister Denny, you can wear this in your little green *sports* car and have all the women you ever wanted.' Denny liked the idea, even if he knew the last part of that sentence was more than he could handle. For ever thereafter, the hat reminded him of her best qualities.

So not only had the driver and his cohorts (a good fifteen to twenty years older than Denny – and they should know better) offended Denny and his hat but they had unknowingly offended Kath. If Denny had a screwdriver, he'd be afraid of what he felt he wanted to do. But this was useless. They were jerks and he was in it for the transportation. He tried to pretend he was baggage, absorbing the bumps in the road and the taunts. He watched the rain pelt the windshield and flatten out, only to splay and flail like a barb – taking the throat of the conversation with it. But where there was one streak, there was another to follow. All the drops flailed and felt the way Denny was feeling, taking the wind out of him while it did.

'Bet you're the real deal, huh, mate?'

First of all, don't you call me 'mate', Denny thought to himself. He didn't reply.

'It's a sick toupee! I want one!' the blonde woman in purple London Fog claimed.

Denny said nothing. He knew they were pretentious and they could say anything they wanted. He only needed to get to the next town.

He thought he'd better think of something far away but imaginable, to still the riot of narration blurted at his expense in the car. He decided he liked roller girls but he liked best ones in puffy sweaters. This gave him a happy thought. The girls' roller derby was too rough for him to watch but, imagine, he told himself, if the whole thing were softer, in slow motion, with hugs instead of hits, a waltz of cats, a spinning of cotton candy, warm – like socks on the feet, to be asleep with this kind of dream, to 'bump' into a fluffy sweater and spin to sleep; he'd rather. Through ferns he imagined springtime bodies, mature by summer. What preceded *yes*? 'What' does, exactly. Denny wanted to be in the what of matter, not the why the frick am I here – without a life-vest among these strangers who would never care to know him as he was.

The waves seemed frozen as in an enormous painting of a western landscape but the rain let down in slants, cutting diagonal spurts across the car window. Denny blinked after each one – as if to communicate, commiserate, with the rain.

At the next intersection they let him out, laughing as they opened the door and moved the seat back. He quickly removed himself from the fogged-up interior, realising he almost liked them. The woman in the passenger's seat was beautiful but Denny supposed she knew it too, and this allowed her to see herself apart from others. She must have been used to that. Her man, the driver, was good looking and ironically was wearing a fisherman's crew-neck sweater – as though he'd been the lead in an Irish Spring soap commercial. Probably nothing bad ever happened to him (and if it did, he was skilful when it came to suppressing any memory of it). Their friend behind the driver's seat, next to Denny, probably regretted his participation in the whole event, for every time after he laughed he'd put his head down towards his knees, as if he was asking for forgiveness.

An hour later, and soaked, he entered the same pub where the occupants of the car now sat at the crowded bar. Upon seeing Denny they cowered, he thought, appropriately. This time Mick was with him, and their new friend Nuala, Sarge, and the Saint, who had returned from his precious outing. It was all he needed to see Nuala. He would find as little as a glimpse of her and the troubles he had experienced with the snobby tourists would evaporate. Nuala could see the passing rainy day in his eyes. 'It's a new hour, Den'.' With this, she smiled and offered him a seat beside her. The lads were just starting their second set: a curious lilting rendition of Boy George's 'Miss Me Blind', slow enough to be a Celtic ballad, the pipes taking over for Mr Boy's voice, the *bodhrán* player looking just a little more disco as he bent over his instrument and rotated his shoulders in a smouldering sort of way.

It was seeing Nuala that saved him from his mood of 'an awful mess' but it was the figment of Kath's voice whose encouragement brought him through the rain to the music again. *May the saints love Kath, and may I love Nuala*, Denny decided.

Chapter Five

He was on a mythical quest and it began when he was conscious. He became conscious, like most of us, sometime when he lifted his mother's veil and peered out like a camper in a cow-field, mud and rocks beside him – a damp tree overhead, his tarpaulin tied to its trunk and a barbed fence-post. The sun splintered his sight; he would see star-gas and icebergs for the first several minutes of daylight. Truck brakes, approaching the circle, were flutes to him. Someday he would go to India, chant, feel untouchable, lose any sense of his body past midnight. His head would feel like a globe, a fish bowl with no more than two or three goldfish – one of which breathed for him; the other two were his eyes, or two eyes becoming one. To be altered is a good thing, he realised, but to lose oneself completely is to scare the life out of whatever you had. As long as the fish kept swimming . . . but his eyes were bridge-stiff as coins, and for the moment one, the spire of desire where his neck would be, breathing . . . Denny imagined India would make him a man the way Ireland made women: fearless through the threshold, accepting of circumstance, and ploughing through all hours as if hell were paradise. There was no hell a kid could not survive if imagination helped in the aftermath.

There was no going back from the dream of what happened in Donegal and Belfast. The soldier didn't know him from a brother, but this only encouraged the lad in camouflage to aim his weapon between Denny's eyes as the bus pulled away from the checkpoint. For a moment

Denny thought this was Sarge, appearing after a change of heart. Mist rising from the green grass and wooded hills made Denny cold in his bed and he wanted to turn the heat up in his dream. Kath was the officer who checked out his paperwork and in a tangential dream she called him to her office, a warmly lit concrete room in the back of a bunker with one slender horizontal window flush with early-morning light saturating her desk. There, standing at the edge of her desk, she unzipped her centre pocket and reached for what he thought was a smoke – although Kath had quit. Lipstick, maybe; chapstick; gloss. The next thing he knew he was in slow motion spinning on a cream-coloured raft as the topaz-tinted sun, directly overhead, made a chiselled vortex of his sternum. He rose like fifty birds had been freed from his jeans. His toes felt he was diving, forward and up. His mouth needed water. He wanted it taken from a heavy, thick-rimmed ceramic bowl so his lips could feel where water, earth and lips, transitioned from the dry bone to liquid. He felt himself becoming liquid. Kath sighed and Denny saw the whites of her eyes. Her breast pockets were widely curtained, pushed like the shape of a vase, and Denny could see no badges, pins, or identification of rank. Pearl shades glimmered in his eyelids. He was hungry for *moules*.

The next day in Donegal he found himself at the centre of an old mill where a projected film flashed across the darkest wall scenes of actors in fedoras, mugging for the camera daringly near a jetty breached by waves. Around him were racks and mannequins with tweed hats, coats, trousers, vests, kilts and skirts, socks. Kath was purchasing a scarf at the register next to the side door. He wondered if she'd wear it around her waist as she did on Halloween night in Rathmines, a sheer black one she'd bought from an Australian girl at a stall in George's Street Arcade. Usually she didn't look the part of Madonna: she was at home in boots and bandanas, over-sized plaid shirts. But Kath had a soft side and Denny had been there. She allowed him for the sake of a conversation grown deeper and what wasn't a smoke now issued smiles and laughter, the taste of lollipop, honey in the hair, toes; syrup in the throat.

Was the fog lifting or was he a dreamer? Could he be a lad in both? Kath surely did manage to have a foot in dream and a foot in 'the big wake-up', as she called it. Somehow she was always so grounded, Denny assumed. He wanted to be this grounded too – but he never wanted to wake up to the sobering disappointments his age felt keenly. Better the fish in the pond whose walls are worlds, whose circumference is a lifetime.

*

Nuala was now the confirmed newest best friend – and everyone liked her, most of the time. At first glance, Kath felt Nuala wore herself like drapery, velveteen stuff around the unvarnished wooden rod that framed her windows. She stuck out while being unassuming; Sarge always liked that about her. She was a real local girl, Sarge could tell, because of the way she talked, her manners, and how she walked as well. Sarge prided himself on his eye and ear for what he called 'the au-t'-en-tic'.

Denny only noticed her eyes and lips at first because when she spoke she hardly moved any other part of her body. She did everything, between her lower lip and her eyebrow. She was a good listener and she said only kind things – even to Sarge, who definitely didn't always deserve the gentle touch. Nuala wore the same green and gold earrings day after day. She'd come from a family prone to confessions, so her nature was good, but she wanted something more wild – as if people, once born inland to big continents, could become small islands – so she could feel as the rocks do. She had a hankering to use more of her body but she couldn't quite bring herself to the place by herself.

The Saint could dance; she admired his ease and seeming unself-consciousness. The Saint didn't have too much patience for people who didn't move, though, and because of this Sarge, Nuala, Denny and Kath tended to hang out together while the Saint was on his adventures.

'He'd do Scotland and Iceland and Sweden and Denmark in a single day if he could,' Kath said. Her frustration was as a result of Anthony never being 'able' to be there when the rest of them made a plan to go somewhere or do something unusual. He'd discovered a world bigger than their small group, and that place had allure none of them could match, not even collectively. She also called him a slut behind his back, a cutting length of disappointment from a friend – for she thought he was funny and she liked his presence in their circle.

Sweden and Denmark and Iceland and Scotland can have him but the bitterness was affectionate, like butterscotch candy a long time on the tongue. The Saint was like this: candied butter that melted in the mouth, a forgiveness given on all things, for all deeds; a smile at the end of a sleepless night. OK. We accept our friends this way, nagged as we get; furious as the kettle boils.

*

In Portobello Nuala was training to become a librarian. The library up the road needed an assistant and the barracks had a spot for an archivist. It seemed the twentieth century was always being mined for what the future could learn from it. Nuala liked the idea of being a librarian partly because there was something about confession that had always intrigued her. The act of *saying* versus denying, the physicality of turning the page between your fingers, the redemption of words inked until read and re-read and faded – which she hoped would be never: these were as good a release as being blessed and forgiven by God – capital 'G' or no; as central to your soul's fulfilment as what came between you and your steamy mug; as measurable as the dream that makes you thirsty but fades before it can be grasped, unlike the flesh, unlike this earth, unlike now. She would house and protect and serve all the goodness poor souls had trouble summoning and sustaining. If she could be their watering hole, that's what she would be: a kind of nurse for the palsied literate class or for the intelligent well-meaning addicted population, which was most everyone. She herself was dry wood dressed in bedding, and others passed her by. Lamppost. Bannister. Shade. Carpet. But Denny knew her in another way. Anyone who spoke with her at the reference desk would come to have a changed opinion, not only of Nuala but of themselves.

Chapter Six

He didn't think he'd put wax in his ears but maybe someone else did while he was still dreaming. A guardian god of tin morality, probably. He rowed through sight and sound as though he were a kid inventing a new world in his parents' wardrobe. He loved fender and petal both when he was only four. But every girl who ever looked upon him as a sweet kid, because he was brotherly, and every guy who saw him as weak enough to beat was deprived of the knowledge Denny held, incredibly like in a simple sack secret to everything that was once within a clamshell, carried inside the dense gold purse of the first princess in ancient times to ever know and share the truth of love. 'Ah, screw it!' he felt like saying. Young as he was, he'd put too much energy into believing the hard-pressed cider of the stars. It got him down. *A deer has better luck in dead winter finding fruit on the branch,* Denny said to himself, thinking of home.

Kath knew he wasn't deaf to the sensualities of the world – to the realities. She'd been his friend long enough to know when his silence meant his mind was active, and when his glassy-eyed glance was the external indicator of his increased heartbeat and a yearning, earnest and wide-eyed, next to be developed and articulated on his tongue. Sarge could dismiss him as hopelessly naive, although Sarge admired his curiosity. The Saint may be sanguine, blowing past the obvious limitations of time or odds. Denny considered these things much too meticulously. He wanted a bit of what the Saint had. Saving the dust off Saint Anthony's glittery platinum coat as he strode by was futile for Denny. The dust just dissolved anyway.

Maybe over time he absorbed some of that dust. Maybe the grace of the Saint's gallop and leap transferred a fraction of his magic through miraculous osmosis.

Anyone who noticed the Saint adored his style and poise, his charm and gift of the gab. He was a stallion, all right: a white one made for her majesty – or to the farthest cloud, where Michael Saint Anthony had permission to go. The Saint was giddy when one expected this from children and adolescents only. He was super-sophisticated and mature exactly when you thought he'd be too much a kid, a frat-boy in a tuxedo. No, the Saint's smoothness was a gift his academic father bred once the Da started being paid by corporations, and paid well. And it was the Saint's mother who instilled a cultured sense of timing, interest in others, respect for the ripe moment, and a thirst for places greater than where she came from.

Their room in the plain house with the black door across from the leisure centre was an embarrassment of transience but it also suggested their actual backgrounds. The Saint had been raised by fawning, but strict-for-the-period, Protestant grandparents from when he was ten until he was thirteen, while his father was a distinguished visiting intellectual – and later on sabbatical – with his mother in Cambodia. At the same time, Denny grew-up thinking he was poor in a neighborhood of fathers who were never home. His own father, he falsely observed, had to work extra jobs during the summer to keep the house and enable Denny's mother to partially fill the refrigerator. They attended Mass as a duty and made a collective impression that was positive, suburban, responsible, within the class of upwardly mobile, but individually they were reluctant. These were simply realities and not a complaint. Denny felt he had nothing to confess. He was filled with questions, but he had nothing to confess.

His father had been a lawyer when Denny was a baby but Denny's mother couldn't stand the amount of cigarettes Denny's dad smoked then – and there was a receptionist Denny's mother didn't care for either. 'How many divorces make – multiply! – and divide a man's lifetime salary?' his mother asked sarcastically one night before an unusually quiet dinner ensued. Three weeks later, dad quit the office and the following month accepted a job teaching social studies and geography. Denny thought his dad couldn't be happier, but he knew better. To teach geography and social studies is to want to be among the people who became your subjects, to enter the geography you entreat with an emerging trespass and interest. Denny's father was this kind of traveler, who was in third gear, wanting to complete the 'H' pattern and never able to. Who drives a car at the threshold and never pushes through? Suburbia mocked its own participants. Denny wanted to experience the highs and lows of what the world has to offer, too.

Two queen-size mattresses, two sleeping bags, and two blankets from the airline took up the floor in the room Denny and the Saint shared. No bed-frames, no springs. One closet kept two shirts each and their coats. They were fine living out of their duffle bags. A modest student lifestyle, far away from home, belied their better-dressed selves, which they displayed more comfortably inside the leisure centre. The first time Sarge took a look, he was comforted by the barracks-like normalcy of how his friends lived, for he had assumed they were privileged wanks – to some degree – and he too thought he had latched on to an opportunity for eventual personal exodus.

Sarge's upbringing in Finglas prepared him for the Defence Forces but it also readied him for leaving. The barracks was his single-star hotel, and the monthly paycheck was independence and mercy.

'Why you want to shout? No more!' Sarge's mum bleated at his dad. She didn't want him to yell but it was what she had come to know, and the stillness was unforgiving otherwise.

Denny had waited outside in the rain and wondered why Sarge had even pleaded with him to be his accomplice. Sarge wanted something from his parents but Denny didn't know what. Cash for the leisure centre, Denny figured. Or maybe they'd asked their son for a loan and Sarge was there to tell them he couldn't do it. Or he'd returned – with Denny's back-up – for one last memento from his childhood drawer: of all things, a small 'arrowhead' (archeologically wayward as this would have been) that a younger Sarge had once believed, as a six-year-old Beaver Scout, he'd found in a murky brook at the bottom of Tobernalt Holy Well, on a troop stop after a jamboree; he had determined a whole story – the sprout! – on his first real outing beyond the cell of home: coughed out of a lamprey's mouth, the tiny dagger had been rounded into a pebble, like a mottled pearl, a tiny version of one of the ocean's

41

boulders inside the dwarf-serpent's stomach. For whatever reasons, there were loud words exchanged and Denny got anxious pacing a square of walkway outside Sarge's family home, having not expected to hear the muffled, stern voices.

The walk from the edge of the complex to the centre unit was like the long walk inmates must feel when they first enter prison. Denny felt the mix of sweat and rain and could see that his friend Sarge was timid as he had stepped off the city bus, aware already that they'd want to avoid the boys at the bus-stop on the other corner. Denny kept his head raised to counter Sarge's lowered one. He figured someone ought to look out or try to look strong. He was thankful Kath had encouraged him to buy the leather motorcycle jacket in the arcade, and he was glad he was wearing his high-top sneakers in case they had to run.

The girls there were both thicker and thinner than they were in Rathmines, and a few neighbourhood cats skulked about the bus-stop under the bench and behind the trash-barrel. Horizontal stripes seemed to be in fashion, and as cold as it was, the girls wore them with thin straps. Three young mothers with infants strolled past the bus; these were heavier, like back home, in Spandex.

Kath said, before Denny went with Sarge, 'Don't bring her home pregnant.' He didn't know what she was talking about when she'd first said it, but now he thought he understood. Of course everyone deserves a chance, and Finglas sure deserved many chances, just as any part of the north would. Was it pride that fixed things? Exile? Maybe a little understanding. 'Come back with your scones intact, will ya?' Kath told him – but not to scare him; it was to beef him up.

Beef him up! For what, anyway? Denny was glad he didn't know what to do with his life, because if he knew, he'd be sunk, stuck, pegged in a hole of his father and forefathers, and there'd be nothing new. He was happy Sarge could get out of where he'd been stuck, even though Sarge probably felt stuck still. Kath was a free spirit, and for this Denny sometimes wished he were a young woman on the verge of anything. The Saint was stuck but he was stuck where he wanted to be. Sometimes back and forth! Lucky luck. He was the kid. He was the missing piece on the bracelet. He was every cat's purr.

Nuala was different. It was as if she had been born into a place that had never been occupied. She'd get to form her own radiance, her own opinions, have her own experiences – like an orphan who has everything she'd ever need. Only, sure, she had parents and she had history. Still, it was Nuala's to win, and anyone who never bothered to meet her had her to lose.

Denny knew this. Nuala was special. He could imagine chalk in her hands.

Chapter Seven

Having grown up together, the Saint and Denny knew their moods and next moves without a signal. Every morning Denny would run to the bus-stop, which was just out of sight of his parents' house, far enough from sight that he was usually panting as he approached the corner where the driver was supposed to stop. It was like the monotonous maze of suburban neighborhoods south and north and west of the Dublin, designed to appease those living in its cookie-cutter platforms but curved in places to make them forget they were penned in. Who has *sex* in such a place, Denny thought. Why don't we ever see the bodies of the old who must die here, given so many houses? There must have been five hundred houses, a thousand maybe, and unless you had one of the curved lots at the bend of a street, or along a cul de sac, your family could see into the neighbours' living spaces on three sides. When they showered, you knew about it. What they were cooking for dinner, you either wanted it or ran to the other end of the house. Family disputes were not fights but animated conversation everyone got used to, for practical purposes hardly different from the entertainment programs some families seemed to keep on high volume. 'Up Arsenal!' 'Did you see the cover of Charlie Hebdo?' 'Feck the price of petrol, pour some buggered drink in it!' To be so near the walls of strangers was an intimate curiosity. Many sons and daughters dated this way, even – especially – after despising each other over the course of the preceding years. One got to know that the certain sound of a toilet flush was the daughter or the son, the mum or the dad. Increasingly it was only one parent, and increasingly the

44

triangulation of animated dialogue was conducted in altos and sopranos. But it was not so sad to Denny. He liked those odds, even though he knew that, for him, nothing would have come of it.

There as here, the Saint was always ready for the bus long before Denny. He'd chat up the neighbourhood girls who had, or later would have, a soft spot for him. He had a way of delivering a handshake or fist-bump or high-five or shoulder-hug – whichever made the other feel more well liked – with ease and subsequent distance; enough that, by offering his everything and then withdrawing, he had cornered the market on being the alpha-man.

Well, good for him then.

Twice a month or so, Denny would miss the bus. Tail lights would fade around the arc of the next curve, and whether or not the bus driver had seen Denny, that tail was like the high neon rump of the long-legged lass he'd never get to turn around. The Saint would get on without saying a word about Denny, or if he did it was 'Denny texted me; he's late' – which would have been obvious enough to the driver. There was no 'Waiting for my friend' or 'Stop the bus, please, Denny's huffing it, rounding the corner.' Kids had a mean way of staking out their territory while at the same time maintaining their friendship.

It surprised no one (except Denny) that the Saint could flirt with the bus-driver. 'Was she mousy, then?' Kath asked the lads upon hearing their stories. 'Hardly tall enough to steer a bus that was the size of Bill Gates' yacht!' said Den'. (Did Bill Gates even *have* a yacht? Didn't Bill Gates seem too normal for that? But he had a palatial cabin on a lake, didn't he? Who needs a yacht on a lake? Bill Gates does!) 'So she's driving a bus as big as a yacht – 'cause everything's big as Texas where you're from, Den', isn't it? And your man Mr Saint gives her the high-five with his golden eyes?' 'Yup. That's about the measure,' says Denny.

Fook the flirting, and feck the yachts, Denny should have thought. *I've got a ship named Beckett and another named Joyce and they'll rock off your socks.*

But instead, Denny returned to thinking about Bill Gates' house and the glamorous things he'd never have. He thought he'd read about the state of the art sci-fi pool and the eternal surround sound, the space-age buttons that guests would wear to open doors – and confine rooms too, and probably track their levels of hunger and thirst. Denny didn't mind this, although he was conflicted about ostentation. Actually he admired the Gatesean legacy – giving money away, and to the needy in ways that not only eased their poverty but endowed them with the tools of accomplishing all the things he had achieved, and move, if they would, beyond his contributions. A house in the woods, no matter how large, is a gnomey thing. Kath would agree. There's no blight or offensive smear. Nothing in-your-face. In fact, the opposite. There was only space, and sprawl, and everyone – the poorest among us, Denny thought – was entitled to space and sprawl. It was a likeable idea, like a hand extending itself from its shirt-sleeve to scrawl the divine letters of what's for lunch.

But if the Saint had an uncanny way of teasing the driver by *usually* saying hello in the most polite and flirty way, every few days he'd go silent and board the bus without giving her so much as an acknowledgement. It was as if she'd done something wrong. If they were neighbours, Denny would have thought for sure they'd been having an affair. How inappropriate, Nuala would suggest – Nuala of our man Denny's developed interest, a notable event to be as sure as the sauce is savage. Nuala was always claiming other people's behaviours were poor, yet Denny had a feeling she 'kept a well' for wanting the same gumption that enabled others to be so bold in private or in public. Kath was a bit more 'gumptuous', Denny would say. He knew Nuala to be gumptuous in private, if the secret they were to share was to be kept a secret, and if she could be assured that, by testing her toes in the water, she would not be changed. Some people are saved by uniforms. Some people are changed because of them. Nuala, Denny was getting to see, was both.

'Why, hello, Miss Ann E. Hall!' the Saint would occasionally say to the sweater and blue eyes behind the wheel, her seat propped up as though she were sitting on books, the pedals seemingly extended to meet her short reach. 'Miss Hall' – or 'Haul', as it should have been – smiled a slippery lip-gloss kind of smile that no lad before his Leaving should see too often. Her eyes glittered indeed 'like diamonds' – and she herself was infused with the scent of a Mediterranean holiday. On Mondays and Fridays, before holidays, and especially on the first and last days of school, she'd wear a perfume that smelled like thyme. Denny thought this was very courageous because it was almost manly, woodsy, organic, but with a little spice. Kind of like Xanadu on a lakefront. The Saint had never bothered to notice the bus-driver's aroma. To him, she was baseball and grease; coffee with extra cream and sugar; snow-cone.

Denny continued to use his bus ride to think about the inventor of ubiquitous digital technologies, and found himself in the imagined leather seat of the lakeside library, a rotunda only smaller by the limits of the eye than the one named for President Jefferson. 'A library should have an oculus,' Denny mused. And there he drifted into the centre and rims of this oculus as if he were a swimmer, a diver with extra breath exploring its vacuum capacity as if he were the portico to fit such a mould. He thought he could appreciate Miss Hall a lot more than the Saint would, although everyone's eyes – including Miss Hall's – seemed to open invitingly to Saint Anthony, without question, as if Elvis were a Boy Scout. He had that way about him. Right: a gift.

Chapter Eight

A musky rose, apricot snatch, picked lavender, pressed under thumb to the nose of brain-matter: infusion of bicycle pedals and chains pulling rubber filled with air; a kind of liquorice, grinding out a root, surfacing on a new planet. Who needs heroin or any other synthetic crap for that?

Kath and Sarge somehow barely avoided the draft of misbehaved conscripted dorks and deniers, feigned cool kids and outliers, liars and the lambasted, the overlooked and the be-damned, the ne'er-do-well, critically shy, implosion with emotion, merely average avengers – in public, those private commandos of pathos and inspired antics. Maybe inside they trusted they could be whatever they wanted to be.

If they had a flag, it was of three kinds of lips, fit for a band poster – made of jalapeño, ash and fire – and you could hear the electronic bass-drops and drum-crashes like the aftermath of war, or a memory of birth in a season of troubles – an ensuing flute flapping the cloth into wind snaps – pop, pop, pop – and a different kind of gun. The lips always win: that's what Kath said, and she ought to know. There's nothing bad about knowing. To know a few things either closes you up or opens you wider, and either way your lungs get bigger and you feel your body snuggly the way an anchor feels the sand, the way a tree knows its trunk can withstand most gusts and brutalities – climbers, carvers, lightning. It's the way a ship with a mythological or literary name becomes the library for every peaceful soldier. One always drifts towards mermaids and muscles, mussels and cream, golden tea and sunlit hairs. What shines becomes the lucky coin – and most of us want it only to spend it.

'Let the Sisters of Mercy keep it,' Denny said to himself. Poor Marian Hall, poor Milltown. 'The Sisters could use a coin in their pockets.' He'd been walking the trail in search of no one, and no one was in search of him. An auburn hedgehog scuttled thirty metres ahead of him, its hairs spiked and glistening.

'Ah! *Dun rua*! A mercy run from the Sisters?' Denny called out to it. He thought of the chestnut gelding Kath told him she obsessed about as a girl. What was it about hairy things that run? Perhaps Denny should dye his. Maybe he should be running the trail instead of walking it.

The water looked cold this time. How many bridges, how many bodies? The kid in the car, the firefighter. No wonder the River Slang entered it. Still, Denny thought – with reverence – living along the Dodder would be an appropriate place. 'Closer to the *slang*,' Denny said aloud, toying with language as though it were a river. It was a bit of an epiphany, the thought of living anywhere closer to water, as if walking through air wasn't enough. You take your chances anywhere. 'Meditate on that!' Sarge might say as he was sinking the last shot. Denny might as well take his chances from Three Rock Mountain and tidal floods. It would be good just to be closer to the water.

In wet weather, while other people in the city were shopping in the malls for the holiday, Denny sought a little solace under his hood and remembered the drive under the railroad bridge back home: how one side had to pause so the other could enter. It looked sexual to him, even then. The big arched walls of bridge girding the track, traffic entering in a stream, the other side waiting as water's weight building behind itself, the hands-over-the-ears 'whoosh' of being held or under covers or inside something with rounded walls.

A woman in beige Spandex pants, heather purple UCD sweatshirt, and dark hair tailing out of a gray slouch beanie was running along the trail. She reminded Denny of someone he'd seen near his grandparents' house when he was sixteen, and starting to notice the larger world. They were both in the prime of their lives, as older people would like to point out. But he pictured a young mother with two in the sandbox and one in an infant swing on the porch, bent like a pitcher in summer's grey shorts and a white Spanish blouse. She seemed too young to be a mother. She could be Nuala, coming from a different direction. It could be Kath.

He remembered the day, the raw feeling of being sixteen. Back then, a few houses away, there was the red plastic Santa nailed to the top of the fungal blue trailer home, like a little pine tree the builder had set to pay tribute to all the builders before him – and to the trees, a sort of ironic 'thanks'. Over the rise of road where the county sheriff was overseeing the planting of a community garden several acres long, the prison's white van windows all blackened, inmates on their knees appeared to pull rocks from the soil in futile prayer. Several enormous clouds, tens of times larger than stadiums, sprayed themselves a kind of mural against the robins' infinity, turning vaporous sails into fists. His own home was a rough combination of agriculture-meets-crimes-of-boredom, the industrial past lost to crumble and a shift to differently produced materials, the brain-drain of not enough paying jobs for lots of children born around the same excited sloppy time when their parents paid spit for fuel and spit for a mortgage. 'What would we have if we had anything to attempt to have?' 'We' didn't quite know. 'We' played on with gadgets that looked more like toys, and girlfriends and boyfriends who acted like exaggerations of their fourteen-, fifteen,- sixteen-year-old selves.

Ring a ring of roses. Every month in a year was rare if you tried to stop the clock, and Denny felt he was getting *auld*.

Yes, they could make it in the cottage. Yes, they could be a couple. Yes, they would pick up and go if the river flashed – but probably they'd be the rhino. And it was OK if he didn't fit in. Maybe he'd never be *golden* and he'd always be an immigrant, but he thought he could stay – and maybe carry on what the Saint couldn't have. Or maybe just be Denny, with Nuala. The river would tell him when to go.

Hand-mixer, towels, sugar. Frosting, rhubarb, strawberries, flour (cake), water. Nuala's 'take out one stick of butter from the fridge and let it soften' seemed to conjure a pent sensation Denny hadn't experienced since geometry class, when the math teacher was also leading the cheerleading team. She could say her ABCs, and Denny would find a cove and a raft. Mint tongue through a raspberry centre, to Denny she could tie clover and deliver tiny buttons.

A soundtrack raced figure-eights around Denny's cranium and snow – or he thought it was snow – tickled his skull underneath his scalp, on the *inside* of the bone, a kind of bee caught in the thin space above Denny's too-packed underwear drawer at home. All sensations perceived with equal attention at his age, he began sorting them, one by one, and which ones – he decided – would get the crown for *again and again* status would make themselves known to him like Nuala's way with butter.

Such is a boy's life. So say the girls? Who cared whether fitting in was personal or public; it was the fitting. It was the *in*. It was usually a matter of buying satisfaction, which – it turned out – you *can* buy. Sometimes. When you're desperate. Perhaps all the time. Sheet knows.

After the rain, more people noticed the river because of the sound, especially near the hems, the weirs. But otherwise the brown snake curled and wrapped, then stretched and held, the southside of the city unnoticed. It was like the elastic around a leg, the belt worn through loops season after season, the hair band lost in the craze of eyes and mouths too full of craic or sombre study. He wanted to hear the *um* and *em* because of it or through it. He wanted just before and just after the laugh as well as the laugh. He wanted the whole migration of moans, from drenched-in-rain to the-body-running, a pant and then a breath, an awareness of himself as having been once a kid and now individual in the middle of life-decisions that were no more special than the flow of a river or a fall of rain. What was inside him was inside the runner. The elastic he didn't feel was the elastic she didn't feel either. The swans in the river around the bend were only swans to themselves but the river gave them a chance. We run around it. Drive without stopping. The rain adding to what the mountains sent, and to anything the tides have to force in, buoy the bulky chocolate up from the underside of south Dublin, its own slang creeping in like a tongue that speaks no words but is an ear to *um* and *em* and other sorted strains of delight – like the world depended on it, and no one noticed.

Chapter Nine

He only needed to decide to stay. It was the opposite of what the Saint would do, but to Denny, staying in Dublin would allow him to grow up a little. The flat along the Dodder river, closer to the city centre and to the sea, would provide Denny – and Nuala, more and more it was looking like – the chance to take a chance.

The worker's cottage was clear enough for Denny to get through, but about half a dozen or so pots and groups of starter spuds remained. Yet he was able to begin to envision a studio. Living on his own would be a mental and emotional relief, he thought. He realised this as he was sweeping little heaps of dry leftover soil – mounds like tiny breasts, light as coffee grounds mixed with clay, shards of glass, and the dainty rigored remains of a spider – and that the chipped grey paint of the concrete floor was becoming clearer, like his thinking.

The trees out back smelled like Glendalough. There was even one that was bent like the live oak that Kath and Denny had 'discovered,' saved by the cemetery – where crows and red-tails traded turns, gathering around the crown, spotting breakfast, lunch and dinner.

The red leaves were less red and more like clay. What leaves yellowed did so like fabric – like lace that had been there for decades.

Autumn was different in Dublin than at Denny's grandparents' in northern New England. What was 'drab' was really a burlap beige that covered everything. Twenty shades of beige. Hmm. It appealed to the black and tans, maybe. December's black sock would conclude the year, almost without exception. Except for the bright box of tangerines a relative sent from Florida. And walnuts from California, dates from the Middle East. Kath said the walnuts looked like – oh, never mind! Sarge was always intrigued by the thought of dates. Of course the market where Rathmines became Rathgar, Omar Clemen's, did have fresh dates – and something *like* tangerines, for that matter – but there was a social advantage to being able to tell neighbours and co-workers, 'Oh, I just don't know what to do with the parcel of *fresh tangerines* my cousin Nilda sent on from Fort Meyers – that's Florida, you know . . . .' The December holidays were one time all winter when, through the predictable rain, any brightness – a girl's red scarf, a lad's neon basketball shoes – altered chronic indifference into full-on daydreaming about ads for person-to-person travel, but not service-related travel – not at all like the social justice of the 1960s – rather a millennially self-determined justification for deserved travel to the Caribbean; the richer ones went to Australia or Brazil. Down-unders sounded like a pretty good rescue as the rain poured aslant in chain-linked curtains of nails. The magazine ad looked increasingly vivid in baby blues, a white bikini band-aiding a hot dog.

It was the autumn of colours in a city Denny knew he had to search for colors. St Stephen's Green maintained an unusual amount of green, as did Merrion Square, Phoenix Park and Ringsend – to such an extent that Denny guessed the green brigade must be midnight's wee people. It seemed the cricket fields got greener, in every kind of weather. The sudden loss of colour, besides brick, beige, black, grey and green, seemed to affect Denny more than lifelong residents of Ireland. He searched Grafton Street and the Georges Street Arcade for signs of India and Christmas. Here he was, a boy in Araby, glad he had found a rusty bicycle pump in the wiry grass. It happened that this was the season of colourful pop stars: purple velvet Prince and his 'Purple Rain' played on O'Connell Street; old-timey Falsetto Red, with the singer's silly ringlets and a shy but inviting embarrassed freckled face, punctuated the air from Henry Street to Talbot Street, Nassau Street to Grafton Street, and this didn't fade until the waves of Sandymount or Strandhill hissed the bounce of new fame away – to where travelling became lonely again. Like on the bus. 'Earbuds saved me, Den,' Kath confided with a sly smile that belied her hustling *take-no-sheet* countenance.

The Poolbeg lighthouse shot up like a young thing you don't talk about, extreme red fire hydrant, the final heights of man on a thin time-line, sitting on the South Bull as the unseen sirens within the Isle of Man passed by. How Denny wished he was a horse ridden by the wide ring under the loose hoop of a duchess; the horse's eyes and nostrils flared, the back hair coarse but wet and leathered by the will to exceed trot and canter into a gallop. Originally a glass disk the size of a shield bent and illuminated a candle – and it was what that candle gave that a sailor saw. It was no less erotic but also lonesome in Nuala's eyes. She knew just what Denny was thinking. South Bull was like its own isle of man. A thin cord connected Poolbeg to Dublin, and to Ireland as an island indeed. Ol' red was a bit of a bloke, forever signalling and getting in return nothing – save for the lives of sailors and the loves of sailors on shore. Beyond the red was the green and the blue, although at times a person could see nothing but light or the thumb-stub of red as if it were the only thing that remained on the planet.

How is it to feel like an 'only thing' that has remained? It ought to feel like a bit of privilege. Denny wondered if he'd said everything he wanted to say to the Saint – and to Sarge, for that matter. Probably you can't say everything because new things are always needing to be said. That's the lousy thing about going away. What you need to say and what you've already said can't complete each other, they're just *there*, like a hovering thumb, red – made ready.

A sad scrap of a young man passed Nuala and Denny, wearing an 'Occupy Dame Street' T-shirt. The red letters on the black shirt were distinct enough under a leather jacket that looked like it was made for a twelve-year-old. Denny had seen the shirt before. He had wanted to buy one. He'd visited the camps and wanted to sing along with the trad group and the onlookers holding beers and cameras.

A little voice welled up in him. He wondered why it was easier in choir – when he went to church, and why it was more fun in chorus – when he was in school. The kid reminded him of himself, all right, but he was scrappier, as if 'This is what you would have become, Denny, if you'd stayed so damn mopey. If you hadn't met Nuala.'

The jacket was now moleskin. Any slickness had gone to ground. The lad was wearing all that remained above the skin: a little bit of turf between skeleton and rain. Denny had wanted the shirt because he thought he'd cross out the 'Street' with permanent marker and leave it at 'Occupy Dame'.

Maybe this was for Kath. Kath would have gotten a chuckle out of it and congratulated Denny on his fine thinking. And he could have 'one-upped' the Saint, whose occupation among the dames was in deed. And Sarge would have at least punched him on the arm and high-fived him, saying, 'Go man!' *There ain't nuthin' like a dame.* Nothing in the world could bring Denny back, except the returned look of a girl. Not a glance any more. A glance wouldn't do. A look. A real look. Some little unidentifiable intensity there, like the look he imagined again and again at Listons. *I can do this. And I want to.* But every bird knows that, although they can call, they need a return. The voice dissipates. The woods cool down, the rains turn to ice. Denny just wanted part of something, even moleskin would do. Ha, even moleskin would better than do. Soon he was thinking of the scrappy kid as lucky. Lucky to be in the firm step of youth – misguided though the stranger probably felt; miserable as he emanated. Here was this skeletal version of himself marching along like some Halloween hooligan dressed as a steam-punked Pogue, strutting away from the big reddened bulge of the Poolbeg light, not one-hundredth of an inch between his 'Occupy Dame Street' shirt and what had once been strong saddle leather to protect him, and Denny realised this kid was himself – like seeing a ghost of himself but not as a white vapour but as a living younger person – and this gave him extreme hope.

Chapter Ten

This stretch along the Dodder seemed calm and secret, and Denny was glad he had decided to live there. If Lower Rathmines knew the street just above the tires, the new place knew the river – whether the rows of flats had a view or not; there was something mossy and fabled that didn't seem to exist around the flat in Rathmines.

'A little like Georgetown,' he recalled, having visited Washington DC with his family when he was thirteen – an endless walk, then, over concrete bridges and past tall, ornate townhouses. Behind the main shops, rows of secluded living rooms and small offices – those whose customers needed a bit of privacy, like the tax consultants, therapists, or lone artisans who'd been thrown out of the high-rent places along the thoroughfare. There was one massage parlour, a nail-detailer and a Brazilian hair specialist, but otherwise the shops that had their doors open to a river most people never knew was there, seemed more like the back entrances to graduate-school housing. There was hardly anyone to be seen. At lunchtime, the old dikes were sometimes peopled by a small number of office workers who were just as happy to let no one ever know about where they found tranquillity and seclusion during their breaks. Further down, where the river joined the rest of the Potomac, there was a rowing club. The shouts of the coxswain matched the cries of geese.

The Dodder was even more serene and less urban than this – even where it edged up and into the city, like a country boy braving the night-club and scoring an invitation outside of the stalls. Its insistence crept up and surprised itself to be part of something bigger, even if that something bigger wasn't as incredible as, say, the falls.

'You won't find no beggar's bush 'round those D4 falls,' the Parnell barman had told Denny – who, he could see, was as hungry as he was desperate.

'Let me tell you something: the D4 get what the D4 want, and if they want the bloody D8, they get that too. See, *then* they can always say "They *ate* well!" Of course some of us t'ink they *ain't* well! And let me tell you anot'er t'ing: if the D4 be gettin' up and all in the D8, they'll soon be spending a lot of time in Saint Patrick's! And they can lie there with that Swift river that smells like the Liffey once a month!'

Denny finished his fourth pint – which was two too many – and wandered downslope like a sad bow-legged cowboy, using the needle as his constant guide. He stopped at the memorial plate in the median for Augustus Saint Gaudens, and concluded 'all things are possible with UNESCO.' In Philadelphia he'd met Doobie, the one-name sculptor who loved cheese steaks and Jersey shore's rock and roll, prizefighters, battle horses, and Ernest Hemingway types. Doobie was working out of the back-pantry section of an old restaurant that a florist took over – his landlord. His proximity to flowers meant that the studio never smelled like dust or clay entirely, although the lavender did have to compete with coffee.

'You want to be a poet?' Doobie said, less like a question than providing an answer to the quandary Denny was having: should he be a photographer, like his teacher told him, or would he be a poet, or another teacher, a social worker, maybe a librarian? 'We need poets.'

Denny didn't expect that from a sculptor, especially one who earned his scraps like Doobie. He didn't expect to be told what he was, either, especially by someone more or less his own age – who seemed worlds older. Most of the visual artists Denny had met didn't like to talk about their work, and they weren't often complimentary either. Typically, they didn't want to even acknowledge that you could be doing something similar – because, maybe, you could be doing it better. If you were doing it worse, you were a rotten example – and this would be another depressing reminder of why they keep their mouths shut in the first place. No one likes to be identified with losers, not even artists. Yet Doobie appeared to identify with all people, and Denny liked that.

Denny, by now, had witnessed enough of his neighbours', friends' and strangers' behaviour to understand that actually the best artists identify with another person's struggle – and do so throughout their lives. It required the whole earth to turn gold. The lives of the living continue the dead.

And there he was, the bottom of the fourth pint swelling the pipes, reading his old friend's inscription. He felt like he'd been useless. Had he been wasting his time, or was he actually 'gathering stories', as he told people back home he was doing? 'Just another starry-eyed Decemberist?' Kath had teased him, earlier that week. When the music would come and go, as it was doing in the pub now, Denny would be wondering about where the Saint went. 'Where does the "Sli" "go", Den',' Mick had teased when they talked about adolescent things in the tent, when they hadn't scored a lift somewhere north of Galway and south of Sligo. Where does anyone go?

Bet he's the best ghost of Rathmines, Denny satisfied himself in thinking.

Of course nostalgia could butter a cup for any wanker.

Chapter Eleven

What he was he still didn't know, but now he was getting the furnace started, he was buckling down, he was breathing the real turf of make-all-known. *You think Sandycove is an ashtray, Denny?* Sarge had teased him about the 'studio' Denny said he would make, and now Denny was fulfilling his own ambition – by moving. What Sarge meant was that he didn't see Denny doing crap-anything in his American idea of carpet-bagged Irish oasis and brooder's seclusion. The idea of Denny writing anything felt like such a *privilege* to Sarge. At the same time, Sarge wanted Denny to give it a try – whatever it was he was looking for. Sarge sort of wished he'd had it for his own life. He'd been given little choice.

'You can't be sittin' on yr arse to write "T' Great American Novel", you know. You can't assume t' ashtray is your little feckin' tabletop zen garden, Den man! I t'ink your problem, Denny boy, is you don't go out enough. You don't get screwed. You don't know screwed-up. You look like a bugger who wants to be screwed but will never be screwed because you've battened down the hatches! But t' t'ing of it is, Den, for you there are no rough seas because you're never goin' out far enough t' feel a feckin' rough sea! See? Would you know a rough patch if it sat between your lips? I didn't t'ink so. Denny Boy, supposin' you use those two legs, and you use that there coxswain to chat up a Heather or a Mick, or whatever you want to do – you go down-under and she'll be a Sheila. Am I with you? But you got to keep your horny glasses on your feckin' nose. Let 'em slide, for sure, that's OK. But you feckin' let her take 'em off, see what I mean? You don't make the middle move; she does.'

59

Sarge was also trying to get Denny to go out and live a little, if this wasn't obvious enough to Denny. 'Easy said,' Den' would say to himself. 'One: money. Two: attraction. Three: a reason to continue,' he kept repeating to himself – as if justifying his lot. Sarge had a strong point, however. Mister Hemingway sat on his arse at the old Royal, or whatever it was, trophy heads all around him, cool Caribbean breeze chilling the sweat on his pudgy thighs, but he also made himself go out and freaking live now and again.

'OK, soldier-boy!' Denny wanted to scream back – a little. 'About one of those big names you just spouted. You know what happened to him?' Denny wanted to jab back at Sarge and maybe be a little more like Sarge in the same breath, except for the knowledge part. Sarge knew the names of only a couple of American authors – Hem-boy and David Foster Wallace, whom Sarge called David Fester Wallace (whether as a mistake or intended, or merely due to Sarge's accent – he was never sure). One other he'd heard of, but it was only because he got a riddle and a song out of making innuendo out of his name. 'Ah, yeah, and your man Faulk-nher, I bet he's good in the sack!' Sarge said, around the pool table – when it was Denny's turn to sink the eightball.

Denny shot back, one eye cocked up at him, as if to say Stupid!, 'Mr Faulkner's long dead.'

'Well, so is Foster, and "May they both be long in life and in legend!"' Sarge said, sealing the topic.

'Hemingway killed himself,' Denny had to get in.

'Well, f'r feck's sake, what's it matter? The guy wrote brilliant stuff, didn't he?'

Denny left it alone, because he figured Sarge hadn't actually read any of Hemingway's books and, well, because Sarge was right about the ashtray. Denny would do himself a few favours to move well beyond the ashtrays. In any case, Sarge was about to be deployed with 'the Peace Keepers', so whatever argument they could get into about superficial things seemed to cut the edge of a trail against the one that would lead to their missing each other, as if they both wanted to stay and wouldn't yet cross that line. They couldn't say goodbye the traditional way. Maybe the Saint couldn't either.

'Best not to walk wounded and let it linger,' Kath said to Denny early on during one of their canal walks. 'I know, I know,' Denny had replied somewhat sarcastically, 'that's how the cancers grow . . . ' pleased with mocking the situation by making a little nursery rhyme.

Kath caught on, and rejected it straight away with humor: 'You won't wish it away in a lullaby, deary!' And then she had added, 'My, you are glum!'

Kath had had a way of being a wake-up call to Denny. His little fog-horn. His conscience box, or confessional (whatever the priests want to call it). But Denny's point was how do you say goodbye when you carry everything you've accumulated with you, when you're always going to live with the friends you've made – even the ones who leave you? He hoped he had a lifetime to think about it. We all have a few things we hide. We all have a few things to cope with.

Chapter Twelve

Where the rhino was – statue, or figment, or fair dinkum – staring against the wide current, Lower Milltown supplemented the past by maintaining the pedestrian underpassage for the likes of Victorian ghosts and vintage new lovers. Whatever else passed there was prone to be momentary, for to look at the rhino's arse would be a hairy subject for fools and inspiration to the more merry – toward better distractions. This would be even more captivating than the clamshells flanking the entry at St Audeon, 'the size of a human bottom or a mature burlesque dancer's top'. No wonder this gift from the sea was in the Cornmarket. *Yackety-yack, clamshells on y'r back.*

It was as if every other word in Dublin was sacrilege, and the others were confessions of the deed. Repeat this daily and you have a kind of humorous and mild insanity – playfully so – Kath pointed out. Denny felt as shocked as he did at home in this vocabulary. *Always an altar boy, never a . . .*

'Syntax,' Kath confided, 'is the Irish tax you pay with your mouth!'

She was right. And Den' was left holding the lips of words he was only beginning to get to know, like a boy dangling his first few fish: wide-mouthed, gasping, with sharp little teeth. Slime on his hands. *A new day, boys to men?*

Nuala had sharp little teeth, he thought. She was raised a tiny eldest child, and every brother and sister surpassed her. In her Catholic school uniform, where others in her class at least looked like they had calves and heels, despite the catechismic clampdown on vogue, Nuala's triple-long skirt made her look like a blacksmith or farrier. 'Mother Nuala/ has all the eggs./ Begs and begs/ but never a leg./ She'll bag her lads/ in heaps of wool/ but never can Nuala/ bring her babes to school!'

The students teased her when the nuns weren't looking, and even sometimes when they were. Only her classmates knew what they were talking about, or so they thought – because they assumed nuns don't have eggs, nor would they ever show or feel for a leg. The idea that Nuala, pretty as she was, would never land a boy or grow up to bear children, was an insult with little foresight. The others were perhaps jealous of Nuala's winning smile ('Scull on the water,' Sarge would say – for it was genuine, but she took no jailers), her cathedral eyes, petite transom waist, knees, ankles, and toes a bee would buzz around, and raise what becomes honey. Her lips were the dainty purse even a mother could not pry; they took the special balm of camphor and menthol and soft paraffin to unlock – which they did, in the years before Denny made her acquaintance and in the days that would soon follow.

'*Dodder*.' Maybe Nuala would have one some day, she thought. – a daughter. She hadn't considered it could be with Denny. She wasn't thinking about any of that. 'In our teens and twenties, we're chalk,' Kath had told them all at the Wishing Well near the pedestrian cover, where the rhino's arse was a farce in the face of the county public arts commission (comisery, more like: for all the trash they had to put up with – from priests to boaters, old habits versus gentrifiers, departments of recreation, departments of sanitation, departments of corrections; neighbourhood watch). Denny was just the guy she landed whom she enjoyed helping to fit in; and she didn't mind, at all, his penchant for finding her clothes that were a little less than Catholic and a shy sample enough from Puritan. She, with the sharp little teeth, liked his awkwardness and found him adorable. Denny was readily willing to say the same about Nuala.

As the months followed and everyone was disappearing, Kath would visit from her new job in the city centre: an office assistant in Residential Planning. She liked the good fight: politically joking and low-balling her way through bureaucratic roadblocks in order to see a project done that would house a new class of single working mothers, and their families, or to put a new roof over electronic music DJs now defending their hours in trance and meds by way of the latest in national senior dormitories. It was a right fit, even if Kath had to swivel in her seat and dial a friend, from time to time, from her headset to combat complete boredom. She had assumed she was made for the streets and not for an office cubicle.

Fortunately, Ellie, her boss at Residential Planning, made sure the office was open – with a large bay of windows – and that her administrative assistant's desk should be in open proximity to this view too. There were only two walls around Kath, and one was low enough to be her starry plough (an observation she would make plain to Denny, the first time he visited). Kath took Denny to lunch ('I've only one hour, Den') to Holybelly on St Augustine Street, where the Liberties would meet Temple Bar if there'd been no Viking ship to raise a village. Kath wore the same Zebra slip-ons that Denny had spotted in the window of April Sanchez's shop on Crow Street. The radiant green velvet window backdrop made a pasture for the Zebras, Denny thought. This amused Kath, but she quickly dropped her amusement for the sake of the shoes.

Nuala also liked the store but she was frequently disappointed in shopping. 'I get so frustrated, Denny. Nothing fits me. Nothing looks good. I don't know why I shop: it's a waste of time.' Denny knew that whenever Nuala said things like this, it meant she was usually overly tired and something had gone badly at work – usually an interaction with a colleague. Nuala wasn't made for an office, Denny felt. At the same time, he never would have considered the possibility Kath would 'play-work' in an office either.

They were living grown-up lives, except Denny – he continued to think. With Sarge recently shipped to Nigeria to help separate the haters from the victimised, their lives had become more sedentary, but this also meant that they were more entitled to feel bored, whereas when they had all first met, their boredom was without legitimacy. Did they know they could do anything, and stay up all hours, and get away with it? Perhaps they didn't, but they should have.

'I thought you'd wear your black with yellow "Crime Scene Do Not Cross" slip-ons,' Denny chided, in order to tease.

'A working lady slips on whatever it is she needs that day, Den', and it weren't no crime scene I felt like walking in, all right?'

'Fair's fair,' said Denny.

'Where's Nu'lee?' Kath asked.

Maybe they had been modest rivals for a while, the way Denny felt about himself and the Saint, but Denny thought it was cute – and sweet – the way Kath called Nuala 'Nu'lee'.

'Are you nearly newlywed now then, Den'?' Kath could tease back like a predator. This was one thing Denny liked about her: she was a bold daughter of someone's rebellion, and this had automatic charms. He had a way of teasing back: 'Said Vicious!' he'd fire back whenever Kath would get too smart with him or any other person for no good reason other than the fact that, as her dad told her, she had 'the bite'. (See, he knew Kath had a soft place for the antics and music of that punk maniac Sid Vicious – even though she took Freddie Mercury's side when it came to 'humanitarian' arguments. Denny just saw one more opportunity to spin a pun in her general direction, and watch it land *splat!* What pals do!)

Kath was dating someone they called 'They', and this seemed appropriate to Denny. For as long as he had known her, even in her vintage sweet-and-sour Madonna or plastic alien Gaga fashionista rages, or gauzy peekaboo river-prance delusions, mad Victoriana viper blouses, Sundance cow-girl artisanal studded boots, a hippie-chick floppy beach hat, or just a bandana, the dubstep throwback metal gothy-girl phase that pleased her for a month, Kath had always been sure of herself, no matter how she presented herself in public. Kath and 'They' were in love, and one of the benefits for Kath was: more clothes! She was a tireless swapper, and at times she attempted to convince Nuala that she ought to try wearing Denny's clothes and Denny ought to slip himself into a buff, fitting jumper, since Nuala's colours were so awesome in this department. Nuala protested that she did, in fact, wear Denny's pyjamas and that she sometimes wore a shirt and his favourite jacket. This satisfied Kath, so she locked that one in the drawer. As for marriage, it was a ticklish thing to tease about. After all, they were barely out of their parents' homes.

Chapter Thirteen

Nuala met Denny and their remaining friends in the Garden of Remembrance the next night, which was Friday, because she worked inside the Hugh Lane and it was convenient whenever the two of them, or three of them, or all of them, wanted to go to the Gate to see a play. If it was not the Gate, they met south of the Needle, but that would have been the bollocks, Sarge once supposed. Either the Abbey or the bus-station theatres were nearby. The pub cabaret they liked to attend was across the river, and closer to Merrion Square. *If the bollocks are anywhere south of the Needle, what's Rathmines then?* Denny wanted to point this fact out to Sarge, but Sarge would have none of it. Let's just say the bollocks is anywhere you step down to get to. 'It's not half bad,' said Kath. Kath. Praise her dual nature.

The Saint's stomping grounds were all through Merrion Square, but then again they were practically everywhere. Staying north of the centre for the night's entertainment was safe for all of them, since they didn't have to think about Saint Anthony quite as often there. It would be a long story, otherwise, and they'd miss the living they were meant to do, no? *Home is where the ache returns; home is where the ache returns. Or is home where we let our aches become ash?*

Kath's *They* resembled Anthony a little. Taller than Kath, slender, light hair, cropped. Only the Saint's smile was an easy slide side to side, and Theirs was not. Kath had to press hard to get a smile out of They but, according to They, they had a fully charged domestic life that was upsettingly (to Denny) wild with Nutella and mango sauces, satin sheets and musical notes hummed at all pitches at all hours of the day – when Kath wasn't working. They worked, but on Their own, in charcoal and gouache – selling it at the artists' markets in Temple Bar and around the edge of Merrion Square.

A play would put them out of their minds and into the sensory deprivation tank of another's loves or losses. Strangely, this brought them closer together – and nearer to their own stories. It was sometimes more fun than therapy, almost as erotically awkward as being in the dental chair, and as titillating as hunger right before a sumptuous spread of culinistic exotica, as the mouth begins to form its own dreams of eventual satiation.

Would that Sarge and the Saint were with them, they'd no doubt have a different conversation, perhaps about how the last time the two of them had visited Sandymount someone had grossly neglected (Sarge had drawn out and slurred the words for emphasis) 'to ahere to Rule 22 of the Walkers' Code: *No dog sh-t. Pick it up.* Or else.' Only there wasn't any 'or else' – unless Sarge had happened to see the person who left it.

'It's never the dog's fault,' Sarge had been quick to point out. And hence: a dog's life.

It was easy to miss them. Loose hearts turned hard at the reminder. It took some doing to kick up their heels again, to appreciate the company of their smaller group, to carry-on carry-on pursuing – gasp! – maybe newer (ha-ha!) things. How do you mock life if you don't mean it? Nothing they could do would be so *tan*, or tarnish the Saint in their memory, but they were nonetheless aware of the space beside them. It was as though the Saint had become a statue always beside them, only it moved when they moved, and it was made of air; air dense enough to suspect but thin enough to have never been there.

To be missing someone and not know what happened. A dream montage, a bad one. Colours, sounds, a still feeling. It was a needle in a part of the body you can't reach.

Hungry, the aroma of egg-rolls brought them back to remembering a night in Rathgar, between the lamp-shop on the corner and the Chinese takeaway. There had been a lovely Tibetan bar that was about as narrow as a bus split down the middle. On the right was a counter about as wide as Denny's hand. A barman dressed in lavender from head to toe, banded only by a dark grey Himalayan vest, stood at the far end with his arms and feet crossed. A mirror almost as large as three windshields put together gave the impression the narrow establishment was only slightly bigger than itself. At least patrons had company; at least the lavender barman had an additional set of shoulders.

'That's the bouncer!' Sarge had said, gesturing to the shoulders occupying the most distant end of the mirror.

'Good t'ing,' a drunkard chimed in from the bar-stool beside where they stood, 'he only moves when I need a drink!' Kath could see what kind of place this was but she kind of liked it. It was cute. 'A benign shrine', she proclaimed. They ignored the man on the stool except to smile slightly to acknowledge him. In the far corner, next to the restroom, was a keg and a little prayer-lamp. It was the only place, apparently. Kath, the Saint, Denny, Sarge and Nulee clumped around a small round table that had evidently once been a bar-stool. It was cut shorter and had had its cushion removed; somehow they managed to fit five glasses in the center. This would not have been possible in the days of ashtrays. They felt as close as they would ever be – except for Nuala and Denny, who'd be closer next time. Tibetan music was interspersed with oldies rock and roll – like 'Satisfaction' – but there was also a country tune or two, Hank Williams followed by EDM. They felt comfortable there, despite the barkeep's folded arms and what seemed like a glare but wasn't.

As time turned into new days, they remembered these moments as though they were needed in that hour which was all along going to be their future. 'Maybe Sarge has found a place like Tibetan Bar in Nigeria,' Nuala said hopefully.

'Who knew there were bars in Tibet!' Denny said, and had wanted to say that night in Rathgar. '*Wonders never cease*,' Denny said, quoting his grandmother.

They wished there were a café or bar near them called 'Nigeria'. They missed Sarge more than they ever imagined they would. 'If there were a bar named "Nigeria",' Denny said in a whisper to Nuala, 'what would she look like?'

There were enough 'ifs' to last several lifetimes but they only had one. One each, and one together. One with Sarge, one with the Saint, one with Kath, and so on. If they were going to have only one, and one again with whoever came along, it had better be a good one, am I right? *Ifs* are only for books. *Ifs* are only for relationships. *Ifs* should only precede an action. 'There are no *ifs*', actually, Den',' Kath had told him, crossing the Portobello before his twentieth, 'only *only*, and your only is now.'

'Touché,' said Denny. 'Touch that.' And he had held up his knuckles.

Kath's warm, slightly bigger hand made a flat surface, like the western sun on cliffs they each knew. He could have been in love if only the Atlantic and the Irish Sea could seal a deal in Cork. He knew for some it had, and for them all the bells in Cobh could ring. And for the lives that lived then, and now, how sweet the real deal is – *especially to the sound of sealing it*, Sarge might say, wherever he is – and Denny would wish to say, for the love of experiencing it.

Chapter Fourteen

In Rathmines, 'You sound like a real Tommy Keane there, Denny,' Sarge would say. Tommy Keane was 'the master of des-aster on the uilleann pipes', according to Sarge, who'd grown up hearing it – and hating it – on his father's car stereo. 'You grow to rather like the sound the older you become, Denny,' was Sarge's way of putting it. 'Then again, you like it when you're a little sprig too. It's only them middle years when you want to punk it up or metal-ify or rock the ruckus out of whatever you're feeling – or haven't felt.' Denny'd heard Tommy Keane himself, out at the big house on the way to Wicklow. He was sure it would be a sham, and at first Denny thought the guy who went on for Tommy Keane couldn't have been Tommy himself, for he looked too young. *How many Tommy Keanes are there?* Denny considered. *They're wanting pipes all over the land, and there's only one Tommy Keane – so what's a booking agent to do?* But this was the real Tommy Keane (not that any other wouldn't have been fine; 'it's the pipes is more'n half of it,' Sarge insisted; and obviously his father had set him straight in those early years: it's hard to leave your heritage behind).

The stars were out and Sarge was correct about Denny in those days. He did have a little bit of what someone in their early twenties might call 'a bit of the Tommy Keane' – star that he was. Light and high he seemed. Sorrowful and lucky as Baron St Burren, the mythical hermit saved by Brian Boru Denny and Sarge had made up: his bowl empty in his frozen hands, himself squatting on the rocks looking skyward, rain coming there; the gift of water.

Out at the worker's cottage, under the frosted glass of the tiny green-house, Denny counted the asters, wheels on a slight, almost brittle, stem, five of them. In moonlight they looked to be part of the night, and for some moments Denny couldn't tell which way was up or down. He floated there with the stars, half amazed the aster had even survived the winter. How had he not noticed it before? He'd cleaned the place, swept the potting soil and the seeds, the stubborn bits of the past, the shards of too much to carry.

Pipes lilt as the voice does when pressure pursues the body. The wind around the rocks whistled.

Yes, he knew he could be mopey, and he could admit that maybe this is what had kept him from being picked up — as a friend, a boyfriend, someone to glance at along the streets, or even as a hitchhiker. It was Nuala who told him, 'Be glad, Denny, not a *glad rag!*'

It was the case, long before, when Denny went west with Tropicana Sam — their most rugged classmate — and Denny was eventually asked to stop looking so desperate or they'd never get a lift! Tropic' Sam had a way with the gals, almost as much as the Saint, but where the Saint was high above the ground Tropic' Sam was on it — muddy in it, digging it, frying the crickets and eating the berries and leaves he identified through survivalist magazines. When Denny and their classmate Thomas Clary took the train south to Wicklow, Thomas knew it would be a long two days. 'Denny, didn't you learn anything from camping in the woods?' Mopey, yes. And if you had told him he wasn't self-reliant, this was true too. But it's not every star that gives melancholy a young man's name. Maybe it's through melancholy that young men become the gatherers of names. Maybe it's from this small light, moon glowing through frosted glass, a modest tree forgotten except by misty water, and loss's normally imperceptible gains luminous before two eyes that had never before quite seen them.

Yes, a neighbourhood along the Dodder would be a good place to begin to understand a moon and a modest tree, and everything that runs beside it.

'We've some growing up to do,' Denny told himself. The 'we' seemed to include all his friends, there and anon.

Chapter Fifteen

Nuala saw two ponds. She saw the carp gorgeous and bright beneath the surface. There wasn't anything invasive about Denny. He was the grass and trees and myriad birds – magpies and robins, cardinals, finches, seabirds; he was fitting in in his cast-off tweed and leather cap.

On Canal Road a girl was scrawling incomprehensible words and figures on the walkway where runners were now jogging. She was using EuroStore pastel pink, light lime green, robin's-egg blue, Easter yellow, and 'snow white' – almost as white as the words and numbers on the blackboard in the Portobello café. 'A Dodder trib',' Denny whispered to Nuala, meaning tributary and tribute at the same time.

They were feeling knots in their bellies, increased breathing, and Nuala's scull of a smile lifted its ends more resolutely – and more frequently. They walked back along the shady part of the mall and then passed between the music school and the concert hall at the head of the southernmost tip of Stephen's Green onto Upper Hatch Street. As they came upon the hospital, Nuala saucily asked Denny whether he'd read the post about the fox family that was living near the main entrance. 'A fox at the entrance to the maternity ward? I've heard of that,' said Denny. The corners of that boat rose higher and seemed to pull the knot below Nuala's belly, until the whole triangulation tickled. Her lips buzzed as though they were wings of bees without fuzz or sting.

'We must be getting to be older,' Nuala said, pleased with herself to mark their apparent maturity.

'Or foxier?' Denny replied.

Soon they were past Cyprus and Australia and Saudi Arabia, whose doors were almost as inviting as they were imposing. Soon, too, they were at the statue of Patrick Kavanagh. Theirs was a grand hunger that was formulating a brew they could later name.

'Maybe one day – in my thirties or forties – I'll have a curly beard like George Russell,' declared Denny, feeling the permission to envision his future.

'You mean the American?'

'No.'

'The Briton?'

'No.'

'You mean the Kiwi, then? No? Canadian?' Nuala was just getting his goat, pulling the beard, shaping his whisker with a little wet whiskey, so to speak. 'Oh, I see, love: you'd be referring to the Irish mystic, then, would you be?'

Denny just glared at her. Lovingly.

'Maybe then you'll have spectacles,' she said, prolonging the words. 'Spectacles for your . . . ' (She was being extra cheeky now.) But she'd made her point about being careful who you name because there's plenty who share a name – and wouldn't you be ashamed if you put a label and an assumption behind a name with the wrong body?

'Would it be OK with you if I were a spectacle?' Denny decided to set out in front like a dare. They were getting mighty close to a rhyme, and her unexpected playfulness was one of the things he liked about her.

His losses were adolescent losses. Maybe now he could get through his twenties, get on with his life. Pearl-sharp teeth. Still, 'once you've sized your own coffin you're a pallbearer forever,' Sarge once told him – this time not in public over the pool-table. For a guy who'd chosen to put his life on the line (it was better than being unemployed and living beneath the shouting battles at home), Denny could see a saint in Sarge. He would come home from Nigeria and if it wasn't the priesthood for him it would be 'a respectable analog', as Kath stated. He'd be his own man, like the Saint was, but because he'd been through the struggle and the slaughter you could count on him for his honest opinion, and to be there. He fired the gun and hit his target twice, and that was enough for eternity in this galaxy. 'Maybe the next,' Sarge had already suggested. 'Maybe other galaxies are waiting for me.'

In fact, they were waiting for them all – the galaxies and our friends: the consulates, the embassies, the offices of intermediary lands' relations, the joggers, the kids making maps on the blacktop, the uniform differences between Cork down south and Dublin further up, the sassy ones in Galway and the petulant back East, the B&B mistresses in Belfast and the mothers of the road, the presidents and the tormented, the poolsharks and the lackeys, the affluent and the bottom-maids, the sick and the just-born.

Chapter Sixteen

The Saint's presence among the lost-and-found things fanned out like a radio, giving instant reception across all situations – time and subject. Kath first proposed he'd be a radio announcer, a handheld DJ, a mind-reader. If so, the Saint was certainly applying that knowledge, from wherever he went.

In the months following his accident, there was no trace except in extra-sensory ways – such that Denny wondered if he was making it all up. 'One fathoms,' the Saint was fond of saying. But he would never finish this sentence. Denny sometimes finished the Saint's sentences, before he died and after, but in his own head. This way, the Saint was with him all the time – whether either of them wanted it or not.

One fathoms that when you go, you are all about. 'There are communications networks all across the universe,' Kath proposed. (She'd done a bit of subscribing to 'leftfield'-theory sites.) Denny wasn't about to doubt her. Nor was Nuala, who thought Kath's trails were either cute or spunky. They were both. Sarge thought Kath was always over her head but had to admit that if she was over her head, she was over his too. Truthfully, he admired Kath's resilience.

To vanish meant that he had died, but a saint never deserts a constituency, yes? Over the years the 'radio' signals would be spot-on, from fizz to nothing clearer. If a long arm could write these words then a long arm would, by way of placing it at the back – top of the spine, between the space where two lungs continue to rise the way birds' do, sitting on a nest. Nothing defined the presence of a friend who passed so distinctly as the indistinct – suddenly defined, although this lexicon didn't always have room for the words that might have been formed here. 'We were lucky to have sinned,' the Saint told them the last time they were together at the well. He didn't mean to be religious. He meant it as a point of subversive pride, actually. But it was a fact, and he recognised the relevance – a rare admission of his own misbehaviours and easy conquests.

Radio, radio. Such an old word to use about omnipresent sound. But where in this radius was the place for a conductor? The presence of some vague sense that at times is sure, doesn't reduce the question: where are you now, Saint Goodspeed? On a white table. Pinned behind a head-rest and dream. Where were you when? Where will you be tomorrow, and when will this end? Cue master, gentleman dancer, enforcer of first meetings in a glance. The dial gets turned to another arc, other frequencies, others – passed, oncoming, present, future bright lights when you least expect it.

The Saint grabbed fire and would say his hand felt frozen. He'd hold ice only to declare he'd never felt more warmth. He was a conundrum that way. He'd imply he'd be there for you forever, and then he went away.

Maybe someday the song is given like a voice imitating a siren. The foghorn steals the moan, out at sea. The day in warm sunshine threatens thunder and rain. The animals are quieter now. Stillness prevails. A handshake vanishes.

But there are some distant stars brighter than the sun.

Chapter Seventeen

Nuala and Denny wake. Their eyes are partially glued. Such happiness sealed their lashes in saltwater – otherwise sad, but lonely no more. Their sheets are rank in ripples and wave; morning through the slats facing the western edge of the Dodder, lace sliding over marble, raises them.

'Where to now?' Denny asked, before yawning.

Nuala held the invisible mirror to his lips, whispering, 'Anywhere you'd like?' – begging the question to lead him on. 'Maybe you'd like to lead me to *Dartry* Park,' she said, having fun with almost losing her other 'r', a catechism that used to be the property only of mothers.

Denny's eyes stayed open, the grace of fired clay; his mouth went dry. Nuala had indeed caught him by surprise.

The high-pitched horn from the DART clipped the atmosphere, almost like the squeal from a small agitated dog whose front paws someone had stepped on. It was probably the old 1984 up from Sydney Parade. Denny imagined the green hose of it and the low moaning sound as it slid into Pearse Street, the blue clock not far – dangling. Trains shouldn't be so full of sorrow, and from the inside, Denny and Nuala each knew, the compartments and the thunder were quite the opposite: serene, sensual even, if you were apt to listen and feel; a gardener's potter's cottage on wheels, firm on the rail of something consistent. Like a pub at noon, a train's a welcoming place. Denny recalled the baritone of the bigger Canadian frieght trains that passed by his grandparents' place. The rumble disturbed, like earth and bridge moving – not in order, as if to redistrubute forms that were already fixed and established. But the rumble was also like the universe saying to a single traveller, almost grabbing them by the shoulders and shaking: *Fool, you're not alone! Love's come to find you.* (Ha!) It was good foolishness to be able to think about these things and not have to be out the door to work.

A gauze of clouds panned the already frayed yellow beryl sunshine and muted Denny and Nuala's view of the Dodder. The view was becoming antique, the way an apple's flesh tinged itself brown. The river itself seemed to absorb much sorrow, and yet it didn't seem to mind either – as though this is what rivers *do*.

'Your "Joni" is coming on the holiday of kings and light,' Denny whispered to Nuala, who was now looking more melancholy than before. She was thinking of Spain, thinking of being a spark right out of her parents' home, travelling the world, being a good citizen, meeting Denny, meeting Sarge, the Saint, and Kath. Her own flesh was still fresh apple but imagining the eventual change of hues – be they the tanning of patina or damage of age, sex on sex, and the birth of children, summer's blushing at the beach or the saturation of darkness – she wanted to wink at the world and ask it, for her and Denny's sake, to slow down.

And where does this sorrow go, that's half a joy? Does sorrow return to the clouds like turf burned into a perfume that sends this voice into another's? How is it that something so ancient, done-up, relegated, crumble-packed, forgotten and discarded, smells sweet – like the burning of the long-dead? How is it that this brick was lifted from the folds of anonymity, old earth forming a compact with the present? It was no one's fault; it just happened. What sweet gesture and comment the Saint made; what fresh sass and alternative thinking Sarge's insistence added to the group; what ragtag coalitions they made in the ensemble of one other – in any part – which was what was left them, like snow, or a smooth rock that is a weight of a horn without a head. 'We'd be looking for the balloon of it all our lives,' Denny spoke out loud, startling Nuala's own silent monologue and reverie.

'What?' she said. 'Like you can't hold on to it but you know that part of it, like a handle, is there. You can hold the handle – but the full weight of what it was holding at the other end isn't there. Or the reverse. Maybe it's *there*, in the solidity of air, without the handle – and it's our own weight confirming the silence of what's not actually absent.'

It mattered to Denny, just as the Dodder's water mattered to the river, where the substance of life goes; where it had gone. He knew there weren't endings. He knew there were *changes*. Trailings, maybe. But why did the most familiar things keep running away? Maybe not running away, but altering to the point of no longer being recognisable in their own old forms.

The apple's open flesh seemed to open wider. A dark spot, a polished oval seed, a birthmark on the cast wall of Plato's cave. Warmth melted the juice, and liquid sugars lacquered the salted base of their tongues and throat until the core was snapped, and swallowing fed their middles till swollen pressure was released fast through a pinhole. Water rushed through the gate down at the little dyke, spinning the elm-leaf like a pedal in a fury.

A radio call came out from the ether but it didn't feel like it was a reach from long ago. Under water, the strange pressure from a snorkel in the mouth and around the ears while almost all sound is suspended, or in California, where in the gravel-grass remains of a burnt-out forest, native tools and markers were left 'as if minutes ago', Denny sensed that those who *had been* there were nearer than he'd known. Radio Free Europe? Radio Free Anywhere. Just because we forget them doesn't mean they forget you.

*

When the Saint travelled on, it was as if dreams should be deferred. Michael Saint Anthony was the epitome of abundance manifested, although not in a gross real-lives-of-lucky-people way – like you'd see on screen. But if the Saint couldn't live his dreams, how – possibly –would we? The golden boy's throne was only painted, and now it was ash. The girls who knew him would wonder. They'd look in the mirror and would swear that they'd never live up to who they wanted to become. All that mirror-mirror crap! Would she be fair at all? How can she compete? The legacy of marked time wrote itself in the faces of the girls who wanted to become women so badly they made geography of themselves, as though travelling would go out of style. They never imagined they themselves would be travellers, only travelled on – looked on, sliced in glance; but they would hold up to it perhaps with the armour of their make-up, the daggers of their age's fashion, the fistfuls of hair they'd pulled from various imitators, impostors and conquests.

How can a girl cultivate gladness after sorrow? Kath had plenty of experience in this department. Come flood, come drought, come storms of circumstance or unexpected pain, Kath made glad-rags from decimated suits.

Hey, a garden is made from many ages' turned and adapted soil, isn't it? Lava-spew hardened and held in the hand is a spec of timelessness advanced from the full-stop consequence of the end of time, yes? Snowfall upon a defeated season is code for sustenance in a form later to be forgiven.

Chapter Eighteen

Out in the sweats, the rhino held its heavy head like the defiant hand of The Thinker – were he to hold a bowling ball ever on his palm and fingertips. 'Atlas with horn,' Nuala called Denny, affectionately. He'd wanted to be strong and worldly. (Who wouldn't?) She knew he identified with the 'critter in the Dodder': a thousand pounds weighs a single head. 'You're becoming extinct, too, Denny,' she put out there reluctantly. The *Independent* had just recently printed an article stating that only half a dozen male rhinos were surviving in the world.

He hoped the rhino would never be bleeding, like the bleeding horse. Of course it was too late – but this is why the Dodder's creature is bronze (or whatever it is). *Whatever it is, it's here to stay*, Denny wanted to say. He thought it but he could not guarantee it. Still, life marked itself in *staying* just as much as in leaving. While here, if Denny could help it, there wouldn't be any bleeding. Only the bleeding rose.

Denny held the grinding stone, the half that remained, and its igneous bicep did not refuse his holding and admiration. The smooth place where someone's hand – probably the thumb – oiled down the rough stone's side in a sustained grasp felt to him as warm as if the person had only recently let go. At that point, he felt they were about the same person – a doppelganger, centuries separated by an instant.

Sarge had never shed a tear. Not since he was too little to remember: a first fight, his dog – hit by a car. Would love ever do it? Would he meet the girl of his dreams, and would she crush him? By the age of nine, Sarge started protecting himself with imaginary forcefields. By ten, he could take care of himself. The army toughened him but he was observant and knew from all he'd seen on screen that different worlds existed (indeed different people), and he wanted to see them.

To die because you've been asked to is one thing, and to die because you believed you or anyone else should never have to die is another. Sarge was of the latter persuasion. The army was a doorway to him and he learned skills, but not the ones you'd think. He learned the difference between people who mean harm and the ones you could trust, even among his own barracks. He grew to respect people, even those who meant harm. He decided the army should be a last resort. *Resort!* Ha. He'd seen horrible things that, in the moment, were all heart and gut and decisions; responses – already worked out, and well past reaction. He knew he never wanted to take aim at another person outside of the last necessity of human obligation: family, friends, freedom. Maybe not in that order. How devastating to lose one. How he felt the pummel when he received the message about the loss of the Saint.

It was another anniversary of Flanders Fields, where all spirit was mutal and ne'er a bad thing would become of the soldiers and haters who stopped for a while to declare themselves brothers – and sisters – of likability, of persuasion. People were being reminded of 'that beautiful game when foes were friends' – although in truth the one side and the other were pretty cheeky about their elbows, shoulders and slides. Denny had come across a stone resting on a shard of glass and the whole history of 'the Fritzes and the Tommies' came to be visualised, as though Kath or Sarge had pushed a phone in front of his face whizzing through a documentary of soldiers' boots and soccer. He liked to think Sarge was playing football, and amused himself with the fact that Sarge would gladly kick the stone and pick up a game if he were there. The shard? What would the shard do? Why this was the remnant of war, to be sure. A ball should top every shard, but only if there are lads and gals to play.

And so.

Chapter Nineteen

There is an abandoned house that suggests history hasn't forgotten
it. 'It's Denny's,' Denny's grandmother used to say, back when the
house was recently vacated, knowing Denny was drawn to forgotten
things. In later days junk lay strewn around the yard. In summer the
clumps of grass and free-ranging flowers and berries were so tall that the
junk looked sacred in the rings the vegetation had declared. Black trash
bags showing as much as ebony-black as they would have when they
were new. Curious. Humidity, or the great gasp, or the methane from the
dump a few miles away, but powerful, bloated the bags maybe. The bags
were shining stones, someone's polished marble, some Henry Moore –
the rustic patio version. Whose gardens these were, would be told by the
imprint of trowel and hoe, preserved among the roots of needles.

Denny liked to walk around the junk, where there were old tele-
phones, a stuffed animal, a barbell, the requisite bottles, computer plastic, a stovepipe, something called a typewriter, sometimes a coin – which
was never an accurate gauge of when the era ended on the homestead,
but close. The place was falling apart, but in a spirit of reprieve someone
once tried to cover the front door with wood and casing. There, a window – almost entirely covered by now – bore its beautiful stained glass,
probably salvaged a century ago or more from a church. The reds and
blues, small as they were, spoke about the gardens and dresses, curtains
and placemats that adorned that place among the vital living.

Things go and leave a purpose. Time, as when Denny held the desert artefact in his palm – the one another had held in the time-warp

before him — would repeat itself in the cup of a breast, fish, riverbed. The slippery knees and bulbs! Kath and Nuala would each have their expeditions. If time slipped away, they could sustain time too. They'd *make* time.

Sweeping the remnants of the old greenhouse, Denny made more time by thinking of his friends: Sarge in his camouflage, Kath with her battered copy of Camus, Nuala in her bespeckled nature dress under cottage moonlight dappled with aspen shadow, the Saint with his beige eternal 'rucksack' — dashing off to anywhere at any hour (probably spectacular, and secret; he would have made a decent, if not halfway-charming, spy!). *Maybe he spies now*, Denny thought. The portals to the disconnected, to those whose flights had already left, to any cosmic re-dialling . . . well, they seemed open. Each thought contained a new portal. You could buy time there, just like the phones and cards bought through the touch of a finger. Probe a little more and you opened a new galaxy.

The walk from Rathmines to Portobello used to be like this, especially when Denny got closer to South Great George's Street. He'd made the homes over many times, had reconditioned the cars waiting for the mechanic south along the canal, had put a club where a gadget store, having gone out of business, left its storefront laying vacant, had envisioned a gallery and a restaurant at the turn of Digges Street . . . and he realised he'd never learned the quickest way to Merrion Square. A simple thing. All this time he could have been cutting through, seduced by the rippling, colourful cloth of the consulate houses. He could have had a moment in Fitzwilliam Square but he didn't like the idea of shootings. Though he did fancy the beaded lampposts, in their feathered skirts, the coal-hole covers with their brassy decorated leaf, the spread dress of glass over the doors, and that semi-circle spot where sunshine would be, mooning the prostitutes at night. He could have gone there as he was sure the Saint did, this secret passage, this quickened way to Baggot Street. He might have kneeled inside the hole of St Stephen's where the statue of Mary will say with her eyes, 'Well served, sir?', and Denny would have to say no, not even along Fitzwilliam, not outside Jack's, the painter's, where everything was pretty. Depressingly, not even on Mount Street, where a pepper canister couldn't wake the old boy. Salt; salt's what she wanted. His eyes went inside the iron eyelets like two legs outside the entrance of such a tall door as to make any man feel small. He'd heard Nuala talk about going to concerts there, recitals by students from Ballyfermot College, such as Damien Dempsey, when he implored the Church of Ireland to tame the Celtic Tiger. He did feel a bit like a leper of St Peter. There was no snow but he felt snow falling down. Chills ran up his arms, and a breeze from the west was as rough as winter. He imagined lace, snowflakes like polka-dots taunting him. And there was that huge door. He rather liked the easily overlooked round cover on the street, splayed like a Roman cap. Bagods! He'd have no altar, and his temple would be outside, low down, like the slowest currents beneath the feet of the rhino, but the door would be always open.

The potter's cottage was always open to the Dodder, and Nuala would provide snowflake, and gauze of window curtain would filter the sun. They could attend concerts at the Pepper Canister more easily from Waterloo to Pembroke at Upper Baggot, up along sweet Percy Place, as though they were Dutch, with the water beside them, crossing the cute old Huband Bridge, with its twenty-something stones arching like a twenty-year-old, despite its funereal carvings. They'd considered a balcony there, once, with the roaring falls and the small grassy cove, but it was too far from what they knew. It was expensive also, the closer you came to Trinity.

The curled lamp dangled from the evening air like the eye of a black swan or a looming fiddlehead in an ebony cloak, like a sister's. It was as if Bram Stoker and Harry Potter crossed here, the red and orange brick of Dublin bringing the wayward back from impending nightmares where all else was too dark. What a lovely bridge; ducks pass through. Nestled beside the squat bridge was an anonymous inclined place, one on either side of the canal actually, where shag green grass would prop two at night like a couple's own secret 'yes'. You would surprise a dog-walker or a squirrel, and the rumble of even a light lorry would excite the ground through the stones.

Yes, they could get to the city 'the side way' and miss all that grit they used to like and ridicule south and north of Portobello. They felt grown up now, doing grown-up things, and strolling through the city where no one would notice them, where they could lay in the grass morning or night and nobody would argue.

Denny was sure the Saint had walked these walks to and from class. The Saint was good about knowing his way and claiming every alternative, always a secret. What secrets did the Saint keep here, Denny wondered. Nuala could tell that Denny was going down a path that had been well trod already. 'Should we call Kath, Den'?' Denny pushed his lips into a woolly worm of a shape and nodded. While it was good to walk like adults, to feel themselves a couple in the city – in the sublime of their secrets and inexpressible seductions – it would be good to rekindle things with Kath. Maybe she had heard from Sarge. The radio wasn't being kind to Africa, and they all worried. Sarge had a good deal of Dub in him, though, and his friends felt sure he'd make it through. And if the Saint had anything to do with it, Sarge would be in good sights. The Angel Gabriel would have to rest his wings.

Chapter Twenty

Kath was convinced the Saint had left 'the kid stuff' of this world and had been promoted as a fleet captain of another more radiant – and all-night – galaxy where club lights and dance music was the water and air of every negotiation. From here he could oversee all of their dumb moves and missed opportunities.

Kath swore that a finch on the wall of St Kevin's sang the first nine notes of 'Tempted By The Fruit of Another' – the remix, to which the Saint could dance particularly well.

In those days, Kath would plead with him. 'Be a love, won't ya, and come down to earth with us once in a while!'

Nuala would wonder ('Could it be?'), sometimes embarrassingly – for she knew the effect the Saint's leaving had on Denny. If circumstances had been different, would she be more or less open to suggestion, she wondered. Pop songs and gossip, games and grub. Denny would beg the stars as he never would have begged the Saint. Back then, they never begged anyone. They only wished. Each of them wished the other knew exactly what they wanted, needed, and each of them ignored the simplest pathways: ask them; look your friend in the eyes and ask them. Now Kath could plead all she wanted, and through it she felt she had a daily dialogue. At least a *weekly* one – which was better than monthlies. It was 'all good' and – if it wasn't, the plea was always there to be answered, and the answer was always in the midst of forthcoming.

The thread between now and the short time that had passed, but which was getting on, was always surprisingly near the skin. This must be what the dead feel, only they turn the other way – because they have to. 'They turn and they return,' Kath said, as if to validate the dead in their dying.

The Saint, sitting in his bean-bag chair, gold short-shorts, a skinny T-shirt showing his leggy arms, royal palm tree leaves nodding on each side of him, a platinum surf 'shhh-ing' serenity . . . This is how Denny imagined him.

Chapter Twenty One

Denny watched the Dodder smoothe and ruffle the bank. In a moment he was back in the States, a passenger in the back of a large plane heading to the great American West – if it was still there. Rivers of canyon seemed like a life that used to be, millennia ago. Even this deserted place, time lapsed, shimmered in itself. What was left was a beautiful bone, the flesh and stretch of it too – even in its old nature, which was young again once noticed. It's as if everything stationary comes alive once another finds it and needs it – even if the form changes.

'I get it,' said Nuala one day as they sat looking at the water lap the rhino's feet after a rain. Denny tried to catch fish with string tied to his big toe and a gummy bear for bait. 'We're all part rhino!'

The land below – Denny felt he could touch it – was rhino skin too. The plane was smooth as the tops of rivers.

Denny felt his skin was rhino, thicker now, and he was as much part of the land as any other body. He could end there and nothing would happen. 'The land continues to be the land and air, air; water, if it runs, only smoothes the land and moves the air.' He was trying to work out the logistics, the relative meta-connections, the context.

When the Saint died, the first seconds after were suspended – as if the counsellors or angels couldn't decide whether he should or shouldn't.

'If you *must*,' began one in Denny's mind, distraught and in the cul de sac of a deep too-much-sugar and barometric-pressure-induced dream.

'If you *must* charge this individual with another service, something higher than his stated tasks on earth, then . . . *maybe*. Maybe we relent.'

These were the saddest words Denny could imagine. Who wouldn't stand up for the Saint? Anyone would stand up for him! People had always stood up for him. He just had that kind of smile. He was the gingerbread man. Didn't everyone want to keep the gingerbread man?

Well, no, apparently not. 'Someone's got to eat the cookie or it goes too bad,' the other side said in Denny's dream. OK, so someone's got to ditch the gingerbread man . . .

It didn't feel right to Denny. Why the Saint? Why not him? Why anyone young enough to have 'so much life ahead of him', as the eulogist said. No, screw it all! He was good for any holiday, Denny insisted, as he was coming out of his dream.

Morning was saturated. It rained all night and the Dodder, far along on its own journey by now, was most definitely rising. The rhino's rump was beginning to feel the push of direction, the temperament of external nature of which it was, as the earth itself revealed, a steady part.

Chapter Twenty Two

'Willing or not, we're a part,' Kath had teased once she was about to accept her day job, and as they were realising she and Denny 'loved' each other but couldn't do a thing about it. They'd be friends. The water and the rhino were like this, though they toiled now.

And so, willing or not, the rhino and the water got to know each other exceedingly well for the time. What was sometimes a mirror with warbles was now effluent, a churning story of everyone's *sheeite* stirred up and rising to anyone's shoulders if they stood by the side. Where would the loons and cranes and foxes go in the sop of it? Denny thought about the piece-by-piece nests along the banks and the determination of the mama bird, about the dens and escape-routes creatures had come to count on, about the homeless camp under the hidden arbour – their wet blankets, lost plastic cups, a photograph and instrument – and where the rumoured Slang's heard nibbling the ear of the Dodder – not a *Goodbye, mate*, it's *I need you* – beyond the long yards off Bird and UCD fields, respite from the known and body-counts: a disappearing Windy Arbour back to Farranboley. We make our own nests.

Life behind and life ahead didn't take account of life present. They had their sorrow, they had bleary dreams, they had whatever was left – which was a lot. But behind, while they could see, was still behind. Ahead was a wish and maybe a lie, a figment held as an obsession. What the present didn't tell, was how much the future would mean to the past. The Saint, Denny figured, would be counting on this, wherever he was.

Denny saw the crow forlorn in the field, pecking at remains of hay. The smaller bird had successfully chased it away but now it had come back. 'The Stars, The Stars' was a song he was hearing as the doe ran out in front of him, startling him at the tractor-wheel. He turned off the blade and sat idling, watching the tail become a star. The whole thing felt like a puppet show, except not rigged. Denny didn't mind. He admired the orchestration, if this is what it was, and he laughed to himself and almost cried.

He marvelled at this memory, the way he marvelled at the things he saw floating down the Dodder, and its power to recede and overflow – changing its character.

'Toy boat, toy boat, toy boat,' he declared, upon seeing a flip-flop spin its way over and around the current, snagged only briefly by a twig.

'Even the stars change character,' the Saint had maintained once outside the leisure centre in Rathmines. Lower Rathmines Road was particularly quiet after 2 AM, and the night air was alone with its diamonds. The streetlights closed their eyes – as if to say, 'Too much. Save it.' The hotel had shut down with the tiger's last yawn and a couple more pubs went with it. No one in the southside of the city would be drinking micro-brew beer again. Two seemed sufficient. Three was excessive. And it wasn't a matter of economy. 'The populace knew what was good for 'em when one family built one plant and that served the entire country!' Sarge insisted. 'And what about economic opportunity, brand diversification, competition?' slammed Kath, ready for a debate. 'It's like a husband and his wife: he won't want another if he needs the one,' replied Sarge. 'Oh, I see, so you're comparing marriage with the drink?' parried Kath. 'Yes, yes I am,' observed Sarge. Meanwhile the Saint was getting all misty-smiley and in the mood for munchies as he stared at the stars. 'Some*one's* going to check this out,' he said as he did a little dance next to the bus-stop, pushing off from the pole.

'Like Bruno Mars,' Kath proposed.

'Like James Brown!' Denny corrected.

The stars frosted Denny's potter's studio like lights in a dentist's office, interrogating the window, but Denny knew better, and in time he got rid of most of the white paint that kept him from seeing the stars directly. Such greenhouses should be open to all light, he told himself. He also didn't like not being able to see what was outside his studio when he wanted to know: which limbs were shaking in the breeze, which birds nested nearby, and who approached – although usually it was Nuala. The birds would have to get used to the new shine and Denny would have to accept that the birds, from time to time, would treat the greenhouse like a bath – disappointing as it would be to them when glass would refuse to become water.

He built a room the sole purpose of which was to make a case for his life. He hadn't built the room so much as he had *made* the room, cleared the space, pronounced it his own.

In his parents' side yard a huge pine leaned over the dirt road that was to become paved and wide – and eventually the first in a series of neighbouring streets in a burgeoning development of new houses. Denny could never put his arms around the trunk. It was bigger than even a man's reach. A rare thing by the standards of new housing. A living monument. Up eleven or twelve feet was Denny's first fort, his first bro-cave, you could say, and the pine needles that settled on the rectangular cut-out nailed to two limbs provided a silken carpet, like a lounge of Shriner's tassels. Denny held a batch in his palm and sifted the fine needles, sometimes pricking himself – counting straws, or imaginary money, or counting for the sake of having something to say and enjoying the sounds of numbers. Up high there, in a box, he kept three baseball cards, a special coin, and a meaningful page from a comic book.

The worker's studio probably never knew it could be a library, a den, a workshop with electronics and wireless devices . . . but this is what it became; and the Dodder complimenting it on its way to the city centre, taking Denny's ambitions all the way to the mouth of the sea.

Chapter Twenty Three

The sculpture that took the bullet still sits there at the head of the bridge and the main boulevard to the GPO; the city could never take down a grandmother, a child, a saint. The needle replaced Nelson's one-eyed pillar (and although it glows, no one knows with what; the mates have gotten bolder and the ladies have become more open and fearless, perhaps), Johnny Forty Coats disappeared in poverty and – worse for him – anonymity, only to have his ideas returned as commodities (the Asian markets along Henry Street sold his tell-tale patchwork – this time as the annual chic – as did the fluff shops on Suffolk Street and Dame Street; there was always a little of the same and a little that was different). Along the Dodder, just shy of the lock gates, Denny felt someone tap his shoulder. There was no one there. But there was, if he trained his eye, the top of Wicklow – standing there like it was waiting for an answer.

'Would you be kind enough to tell me the question?' Denny spoke in his mind.

'Under the bridge at Glendalough,' the voice began, 'you'd likely stop and stare.'

'Oh, great,' Denny said almost out loud. The goal was to get to the heights of all he could ever see, just as the Saint did, not to sit under a bridge – and stare.

'Or was mountain climbing for everyone?' the voice whispered, thin as barely breeze. Denny realised that, whether he was having his own thoughts or whether the voice was real, it didn't matter. He wasn't crazy.

Besides, the conversation was good for him. Without Kath or Nuala – for this matter without Sarge also – it was the next-best thing.

'I am what I am . . . Because, Because, Because, Because!' Denny repeated (he thought out loud), a bit Popeye and a bit mocking and celebrating at the same time the old recruitment poster he had seen with Kath and Sarge in Collins Barracks.

'Because your mother wants you to,' rallied Kath outside the museum as she marched 'Neither to kings or kaisers!' as the banner declared in 1916 over Liberty Hall.

'Give me liberty, or give me – ' Denny stopped short.

'Theft!' Sarge rhymed. They all laughed, for Sarge was hardly funny and musical at the same time. Even Sarge laughed. Being a soldier, he'd be no thief. He'd sworn to it. They knew the American's slogans too, at least the popular ones – a fact that sometimes surprised Denny.

And then he regained his composure and centred on the something more desirous. Presuming the cloak of the great and fabulous James Joyce for a few seconds, he turned to his friends as if he were about to confide something conspiratorial and, scanning his troops in the eyes, declared, as if announcing the most major initiative, 'Give – me – Anna – Livia!'

'Don't you forget about the Plurabelle, Mr Man!' Kath reprimanded. Indeed, she was correct – as she usually was.

'There's more than one facet to a "belle"!' Sarge added enthusiastically, as if he'd known . . .

Anna Livia, sans Plurabelle, was not only a lovely long bit by Joyce but also happened to be the name of the Saint's conquest from UCD, a dancer at that. Hard as it was to snap out of thoughts of Anna Livia, Denny's ear turned again to the wind rushing down the Dodder towards the old theatre on Vail Street.

'Fortune takes a funny step,' the voice said next – or seemed to say. One word at a time, Denny received the dream instruction as a courtesy to the mystic frequency he'd tapped into. He'd only been to Glendalough twice, and hadn't remembered the bridge. Probably he had walked over it without bothering to examine its underside. This was possible. He fancied himself a fisherman but in truth that was his father's job. He was being asked to look further and closer at the same time, it felt to him. 'Wicklow . . . ' Denny considered. 'Someone thinks I need a little retreat in the country, does he?'

But there was so much along the Dodder, and there was the city too. His cottage seemed the right hub of both, and Denny didn't see why he ought to leave one for the other. Still, Wicklow was at his back – always looking over his shoulder.

Of course the sea was coursing its symphony of consonants too, around the bend off Ringsend. To his left the Dodder and the Liffey, Ms Livia herself in some bookish guise, got him thinking more closely about Nuala. He was in a metaphysical moment, one a critic wouldn't understand any more than how a neon pricker could replace the spot where a bronzed floozy had been – the re-masculinisation of public monuments, '*sans mons* as sands moan', the freeze-frame of this time seemed to be telling him.

He wanted to walk the Great South Wall with Nuala, toward the lipstick-head of the point. He knew the Saint had done such things, done them without him, done them with the girls and new mates he'd met at the leisure centre when Denny wasn't there, or ones who were easily befriended from the dance studio downtown next to the meat market. Denny was always drawn to the sea, just as he had found something that felt like home out west – again imitating the Saint, journeying with the joy of abandon. What was with this 'bridge' stuff, then? And why always a feckin' mountain to climb or to look upon as an altar . . . in whose presence you are never worthy?

There'd be no dames on rocks or sands of Sandymount, no flirting teenagers crouched by the edge of the Dodder. Today was a rustic day, season turning to autumn – but overcast, not romantic, depressing. 'A little sign would be nice,' Denny mused. He was tempting the gods and the geniuses of the multiverse because he knew he was actually already a magnet for signs. But just then it rained. Not any ordinary rain but a showering that pummelled him and the cacophony deafening all but hiss. There was no quick shelter until he detected a bus-stop through the dark pitch of slant rain and flooding once he started running in the direction of the nearest unoccupied berth. Once underneath the clear plastic bunker, he noticed he ran right out of his shoes. Somewhere near Irishtown Road he lost his shoes to flash-flooding overtaking his path – mindlessly stepping out of them with the help of the flow loosening and sopping the heels – unaware of anything except his face and the scramble to anyplace out of the rain. Almost as soon as it began, it ended. This was not true. If it could have poured longer, it would have emptied a lake. The length of it made him want to both drink a big hot pot of tea and swear off tea for eternity. The fact was, the Dodder needed it, the greens needed it, the ducks wouldn't mind, and Denny needed it in whatever way he couldn't imagine then and there. Was it really true that the rebels and the occupiers had put down their guns to let an old man feed the ducks in St Stephen's Green? According to Kath, legend handed down from the annals of Kostick & Collins, there was no disputing it. The ducks made for a sweet many minutes of pause, 'Like boyfriends when they stopped kissing – ' Kath niggled. Denny wondered if any armies thereafter used ducks as their Trojan Horses. A sad thought, the origins having begun with such peaceful optimism. 'Sitting ducks, Sarge would have said,' said Kath.

Chapter Twenty Four

The origins of things got Denny into a haze and a fire, when speaking of Dublin – come and gone. Nothing Tommy Keane could do would ease the times Denny hadn't forgotten about. He hadn't forgotten, until and after the day he departs, being next to the Saint. It is when you are beside the deceased that you realise they were living blood and flesh, good looks, muscle and functioning organs. Organs! Eyes that have it. Hands that play.

He could pass every charity shop and think of a thing the Saint would like: the golden-orange scarf from Cardiff's Weston line, the uneven lapis lazuli and goldenrod tiles from Morocco, the young man's stiff-shouldered once-worn coal tweed jacket from Kerry, the immigrant's shoe-shine kit pegged together from Haiti, Cuban cigars found in an inside pocket of a vintage El Encanto satchel, a cabernet patchwork chiffon party dress straight out of Clerys, the African mahogany hand-carved gold-inlay cufflinks showing one dog sitting and one dog jumping, zany rabbit-fur headphones, cobra-coloured suede pants, a Japanese desktop-size plastic electric guitar, a charcoal drawing of a woman made with only three strokes, a small photograph of a horse nose to nose with a trolley, Gianvito Rossi knee-high boots from Stockholm, an 1970s apothecary's chipped ceramic duckling – hollowed out for Spanish fly (he knew because a packet was still there) – and a pair of seen-better-days brown dance shoes (a little too small to fit the Saint in his maturity).

Denny could see how the Saint would want these things, but just as quickly as he'd want them, he would leave the thing for someone else. He liked the idea of someone else finding the things he liked. When possible, when sitting on a public bench for example, the Saint would sometimes leave a coin – centred visibly on the arm or the seat. Or else candy – liquorice or caramel squares. In this way he could be Peter Pan and the candyman while remaining anonymous. Denny could tell that the Saint chuckled at this on the inside. A glimmer of sunlight across his green eyes gave it away. The way he took long uber-confident strides away from the place gave him away. Denny tried to imagine himself doing such pocket philanthropy, and it always came across as clownish in his mind: too forceful, too intentional, 'too'. Some saints have all the luck.

The west country proved to Denny he was part of something 'too' also. Too rugged, even when it looked worn and weary. Too complicated, when upon first inspection the lay of it looked simple. And too caring. The earth cared for what the weather brought, even when earth was gnarled for it. Having brought the rain, weather knew half of it would go away, to nil use, to land people could not maintain, to the abandoned tracts that would someday be wells of fortune for future inhabitants. Nothing the Celtic Tiger rearranged was more permanent than the land and the basic attitude of the people who opened their doors day after day – through season after season – to say hello, begin a task, end a night. And not utterly defeated, people rose through the mess and absences like desert flowers, tiny saplings making it in the cracks of rocks, mushrooms on the torn-sod edge of elevated pasture – below which stands no construct for habitation. Here, all vulnerabilities were isolated as if he were the marksman.

When the rains came, what was still there cowered – not out of the opposite of courage but for shelter, as routine, smartly. If the habits of the smallest creatures – the stones and berms sacredly among them too – could reckon the secret of bracing for conditions or letting go, so too could Denny be this habitual. The snares and folly were locked and released as everything comes and goes. Standing on rock slabs facing the weather twenty minutes off, Denny remembered what Tartulla Frank had said when they both stood tasting a colder Atlantic on their tongues when they hadn't even opened their mouths: 'You have to admit, it's good fishing – from here!'

Then everything is strange. The white boat is a sheet covering the body. Everything is strange. The Cadillac carries an adult child. Everything is strange. Ice cream tastes like mud. Everything is strange. Your phone-number is false. Everything is strange. The game simply stopped. Everything is strange. There's more competition for the dead. Everything is strange. Driving is always rolling second guesses. Everything is strange. Visiting the places in which you used to live dulls the snapped edge. Everything is strange. Beauty is sarcastic. Everything is strange. The space around your skin is inhabited by leavings. Everything is strange. Suspicion hides the rose. Everything is strange. It's official: doom's greed hired pickpockets. Everything is strange. Naked feels closer to a skeleton. Everything is strange. What you're doing never has a chance. Everything is strange. Maybe you'll become a mean muthafeck. Everything is strange. Join the circus, eat from cans; it'll be all right. Everything is strange. More breakdowns than an old car with cheated parts. Everything is strange. Wait for the ice to melt. Everything is strange. Measure the span of the dead bird's wing. Everything is strange. You know they'd like it but there's no *they* there any more. Everything is strange. Maybe you laugh more. Everything is strange. Find ways to compensate; extremely mixed results. Everything is strange. The voice quivering calls to you. Everything is strange. Every day is high humidity and waiting for the thunder to shred the rock. Everything is strange. You're a bird flying the inside wall of a tornado. Everything is strange. You spend a dime and you feel the fortune. Everything is strange. Start to believe in this. Everything is strange. Snow never melts in your hands: this is how cold you are. Everything is strange. Once you plug-in your instrument, you're immortal (almost). Everything is strange. Happiness is trying to divorce you. Everything is strange. The End is in everything. Everything is strange. Love the scraps of pottery, shattered and dust-piled; make a pile of dry clay. Everything is strange. You dance like you're borrowing time. Everything is strange. There's no recognition in the tastebuds. Everything is strange. Songs either stab you or wrestle you onto a spinning mattress, and all you do is see purple and scream. Everything is strange. Unicorns now exist. Everything is strange. By waking, you are a petition. Everything is strange. No pay makes Jack an exciting young man! Everything is strange. Jill walks up the hill and fecks the hell out of stone and water. Everything is strange. The only drug is sleep. Everything is strange. Almost the chalk more than the hand. Everything is strange. Hem can be anywhere, and who's to care? Everything is strange. But save the animal taunted and tortured by the household bully. Everything is strange. Bullies are the indistinguishable stars of dictatorships and screens. Everything is strange. Concrete is an awesome pillow. Everything is strange. Food in the trash is stunning, gorgeous. Everything is strange. You're tuned to radio frequency Live From The Deceased, every day. Everything is strange. The taste of food is granted back by temporary decree of phantom winks and nods. Everything is strange. Red lights flashing are mesmerising and pretty. Everything is strange. Being social requires you to speak. Everything is strange. Music makes the most and best love to you. Everything is strange. The end of every day is a sacrifice. Everything is strange. Salt beats sugar every time – until you can't give a shit any more, and then sugar kicks in with a whack upside the head. Everything is strange. You treat bread and butter as your last meal. Everything is strange. Every clerk is your brother or sister or lover. Everything is strange. You have no regrets and regret everything. Everything is strange. You couldn't do it any other way. Everything is strange. The ducks are not decoys. Everything is strange. You catch the foul ball from the cheap seats (every time you go). Everything is strange. You deserve a favourite song when you least expect it, or when your need is great. Everything is strange. The bending branch in the wind is you. Everything is strange. Driftwood altars predominate. Everything is strange. Tombstones, coat-hangers. Everything is strange. Feel everyone who ever slept in the hotel room. Everything is strange. Crosswalks are the greatest things. Everything is strange. If only I said this is a different language. Everything is strange. This is the fear, eternally. Everything is strange. Too familiar, this strangeness. Everything is strange. Even in my best clothes I feel I am naked. Everything is strange. I-You-They-We-One. Everything is strange. Fish, fish, fish, fish, how long's your life? Everything is strange. Thread a string; strike the note. Look into the eyes. Your eyes puddle and you're on a merry-go-round slow enough for you to want but too fast for you to get off without breaking your ankles were you to jump. Wha'cha gonna do? Everything is strange. Smell the last clothing they wore. Everything is strange. The rain cleans the sweat and brings the sweat. Everything is strange. Love the coldest stone; break no sticks without kisses. Everything is strange. Dance it off with scarves and sacred water. Everything is strange. Your car is a boat but you think you're driving it on rivers of highways. Everything is strange. Friends in high places, and friends in the ground. Everything is strange. Acorn nipples and corn on the cob. Everything is strange. The revolving door. Everything is strange. Felt warms the cold skin. Everything is strange. A sleeping bag will not be a coffin. Everything is strange. A book is an infamous last prayer. Everything is strange. Lucky, lucky, lucky you. Everything is strange. Go whisper in the ear of the sleeping one you love. Counter everything with maybe today is maybe someday.

Chapter Twenty Five

The ground needed the rain but if the rain did not find peace with itself – for it had rained all night and the previous day – the Dodder would brim and pour over safe spots, high as much of the riverbank was. 'Safe no more' is how Sarge put it whenever he ran the pool table. The Dodder was running out of stones, you could say. Denny had a sense that safety changes depending upon habitat, season, timing. Sure the gopher-hole fills. Some birds will rebuild their nests. The fish will find their own level.

Denny sat in his favourite chair, one from the street – unfit for a charity sale. The knobs on the knees and feet, the smoothed swells for arms (where fabric had been), comforted Denny with the semblance of someone else's past, to which he felt intimately related. In the chair he was a carrier of the future and yet all things present funnelled through the wood of the past, like bones. From the bones of chair to the bones of being.

A branch reached closer to the nearest window than he'd ever seen before. His was the only light on at the back of the apartment, and because the branch stretched itself into the light's circumference Denny could see the drops, clearly, on the outermost leaves. The beads were still as ice and smooth as small snow-globes magnifying their green. It was as if all creatures responded to the rain, and the tree was no exception. Earlier this day Denny had read a report about scientists who attached microphones to plants. When a research assistant was asked to crunch on a leaf of lettuce, the plants were heard screaming. 'This is what it feels like to be a plant: caterpillars make me nervous.' Or this was the essence of the article. Now Denny saw the branch itself behaving as a horse might. It was curious, hungry even, and the length it travelled was less like a stray than like a suitor, a shy one asserting itself. 'Maybe *branch* is leaving me a message,' Denny acknowledged, for there was intentionality that seemed too centred on being there, in these moments, and to be without a message could not have been the case.

The universe reached, every now and again, as if to tap the living on their slumbering frames in barely concealed tones to remind them that, despite mortality, there are many levels at work and once in a great while we may perceive the leap and the challenge of the immortal. Denny could only smile and stare at the branch, wet in its luminous drooping – nodding like a colt who gets the joke of barriers. They agreed to be mutual admirers whose arm's span was separated by only a white wall and an open window. He'd go to sleep assured that his friend would not be the same by morning but that, by proximity, they'd met some obligation – transcendental, galaxial. A matter of verse.

Awful as the Dodder rose, by morning a settling had happened; light was light upon a wider swath.

Why didn't the Saint invite Denny on any of his little trips? After all, they were roommates. He wanted to be the Saint and seal it too? Saint no crime? Would Denny have treated his friend differently? A chance to dine with queens, the velveteen underground of the Irish creative economy: Fagin's cross seas, cousins and the rough privileged nephews and nieces of a nation's international stars of stadiums and screens, dragkings, the ambassador of Switzerland's twenty-year-old daughter and her cavorting friends, the gaggle of architects who thought of Dublin and Galway as their beach. The Saint was not Denny's twin. There'd be no way of entering through those social curtains without feeling the blowback of pedigree inferiority. Denny felt like the apartment dog: there when the Saint left, there when the Saint returned. But the Saint was never in their three rooms for long.

He realised, thinking about their shared flat on Lower Rathmines, the Saint had been taking a shortcut, Leeson Street, all the while to cross the canal to class, since their first long walk together along the sullen bends of Camden. He'd figured it out, all right. The Saint had made a determination as only the Saint could – and to Denny's incorrigibility upon realising it, or naivety all the while, the Saint hadn't mentioned it to Den', who was routinely late. All Denny knew was that the Saint somehow woke early and appeared in class well before Denny. How the Saint figured he could accommodate a new city by imposing a strict geometry from point A to point B must have been something his mother or father had taught him, or some knack of being in a city Denny envied. Denny wished his mother or father had taught him these things, although they never travelled to cities – always only to camps. He could pack a light suitcase, rolling his clothing into the smallest burritos and cigarettes, but he could never seem to get to the classroom more than a minute early, and often quite a few minutes late. It was embarrassing. Denny considered himself a good student, a more attentive one than the Saint, at least. But it was as if the Saint had the power to teleport himself from Rathmines to the Georgian rows nodding to Leinster House, like young Arthur receiving Excalibur from the Lady of the Lake. The Saint would have appreciated the analogy too. No, Denny's myth would be the Rhino. Steadfast, but no edges to cut steel. He merely wondered why the Saint never invited him. Was there someone along the way? But if there *was* someone, why wouldn't Anthony invite Denny to meet them? Just solitude? 'Roommates aren't roommates forever,' Kath reminded Denny.

'Even in Rathmines?'

'Especially in Rathmines!'

In this way Denny felt a little ashamed. After all, if he was to be an artist, shouldn't he be taking a different route each day, just like the Saint? Denny started to convince himself that he was 'getting to know the neighbourhood real well', and this accounted for his boring consistency. In truth of fact, it was a matter of his own insecurity holding him back. Fortunately, there was Listons.

The usual route took Denny longer – a fact he didn't realise until the term had ended – and it had the effect of getting lost – knowing it as well as he did by then. Part of him had to keep making it feel new, and so he invented reasons to delay himself along the way. A window held minutes on end. He could get past the fact he and the Saint weren't roommates any more, but it was as if the Saint's absence in life made Denny think about him all the more: when a friend takes chances, they either go on forever or they've had their last chance. The Saint was from the first group, Denny thought.

Chapter Twenty Six

Days, days, and days. It was not only their group; would-be life-time mourners included competing old girlfriends sweet Colleen, mighty Myrna, Cat-the-Fantastic, Nouveau Noelle, a brother in New Mexico, and mom in Texas. It would be a college, too, and a high school, and elementary-school teachers, the librarian, colleagues of the Saint's parents, the cousins and the grands remaining. Denny sat in the far corner of Listons, at first thinking a doughnut would be enough to relieve a pang he thought was only passing hunger. 'The point was to pay attention,' Kath rightly told him one day. They'd been walking the Grand Canal for what seemed like months, and Kath was getting tired of Denny's self-pity.

'Den', remember the songs by your favourite band?'

'Which ones?'

'Dopey, it doesn't matter! I'm talking about when you used to sing so silly on the bench outside the Fathers' residence, you made us laugh with candy in our mouths.'

'Howard Jones?'

'Maybe Howard Jones. Phillips. Icelandic Cowboys, Peppered Persians, R. feckin' E. freakin' M. The velveteen purple plush Artist Formerly Known as Prince. Tracy Chapman, Sinead O'. You know!'

'Depressed Mode?'

'Yeah, sure: Depressed freckin' Mode. The Candy Factory. You name it.'

'No one is to blame?'

''Zactly.'

'And so the bands?'

'The bands sucked mud first, so you didn't have to, Denny!'

'There's mud in the earth after it rains,' Denny asserted, as if this absolved him.

'And you don't have to go there, mister. Some things flow all by themselves, you know.'

Denny had watched the Dodder enough, just as Kath and he had been the canal's accountants stroll after stroll, to understand what she was trying to tell him. You don't go down to the river's edge when the river's overflowing. You don't stay long on the bridge when the logs are riding rockets. You sit, maybe, and you swoon, maybe, and maybe you pick yourself up and walk more, or you call a good friend. This idea – *you call a good friend* – unfortunately got him thinking about the Saint again. Every thought cycles back to its referent, try as we do to phase out a point of mishap or altercation. A fish on a line is still a free creature, but free only to move about on a quickly descending clock; sooner or later someone calls it up, tugging at the test, or else it snaps – by will of one creature or the other. And by will. By intervention of luck, or currents, or through a confluence of raw decisions formed by hook and desire, by witlessness and by ascension.

Listons had changed, some, but the feelings were still there. The chalk, one person's hand or another, the menu, the strange and sometimes alluring people who frequented – especially at lunchtime and just after work. Certainly the coffee was still good. Listons sent remediation to Costa Rica, Kenya, Cuba, Haiti, Jamaica and Sumatra once a quarter as part of the United Ambassadors of Good Taste Club. But Denny still looked for that soft dream of a hand, writing its way into his life by way of black and white. The extent to which Nuala embodied this was an open and curious question. It did and it didn't matter. The hands that come to us at certain ages are hands we remember – surrendered or not. Somewhere in the history of cities that were once merely towns is written the unspoken stories of the sordid and the sweet, the truculent and the patient.

A handsome young couple pulled two chairs from a table and seemed to cover their embarrassment at the grating sound they made as the metal bottoms scraped the stone floor, by taking pleasure in it. They were 'set' – upwardly mobile, as they used to say – perhaps having just come from a friend's wedding. The young woman's black and white dress played carousel horses around Denny's mind, and the pressed tweeds and laundered shirt of the young man signalled something Denny could be, or hadn't, become, or would never assume, professionally or otherwise. He was always waiting for that Galway girl, even in Dublin – even in Deluth, Tampa or Seattle. They could have been in a café in Rome or along the stairs beneath the Parthenon in Athens, in North Beach or South Beach. Denny felt the Dodder rise up, and he was having to keep away, for Kath's sake – and because he'd been too long in the rain. Listons, though, provided the aspects of a sunny day that were instantaneous: the young woman's way of walking when she bussed her empty plate, the clerk's coy warm frame after a day's full shift, the pearl sheen of porcelain. It lifted Denny. And it also made him think of the Saint.

What our friends are missing once they're beyond. Shine – of anything. The wholly vital presence of a clerk, not virtual. The absences, having a place there. The rose which sets its head on the table.

Chapter Twenty Seven

Frying onions, garlic and thyme, Denny and Nuala succeeded in making their small kitchen an aroma haze. The white tile that matched Nuala's former school blouses, the first items to hang in their bedroom's modest closet, looked distant through the steam of cooking. Their bedroom was wide, and three nearly floor-to-ceiling windows allowed morning light through the original panes. Because the building was old, the original glass warbled in some song stuck in 1917. But this wasn't bad. In fact, Nuala liked how dreamy the day appeared when she looked into the yard. Normally one for clarity, she sought clarity in her daily thoughts and conversations with Denny. On the job she was an ace, a top-notch worker who was always happy to bust a pace for the efficiency of a project, knowing that at the end of the day she could leave, and skim stones with Denny.

Back south in Bray, a white boat bottom faced the sky. Whomever placed it at rest had to hike up the pebbled beach knowing it would be a week, maybe, before they'd get back to what they had been doing. What they had been doing belonged to the centuries. Homer's Ithaca, a pauper's profits at Portofino, the disputed Galilee, the sloppy pilgrim's Provincetown rescued by Portuguese, Big Blue Babe's Huron, Innisfree's button in the Gill, ship ashore at Isla Negra, up Paternoster's past-present persisting; even Kinsale, like Port Isaac, from within the cove: doing, live, secluded, together – it didn't matter, and does. Certainly the Dodder held its little paper boats, the aspirants crumpling multi-pointed coracles as gifts to the gods of dithering. Kath and Denny had had their share, messages not even in a bottle.

The aroma of onion and garlic mixed into a sweet, unlikely intoxicant. In an instant, Nuala was in the cool title kitchen at Paternoster with her family. Her father's business sent him to Cape Town when she was nine going on ten. The Grecian white plaster buildings and hip wide painted boats, the crayfish and squid; long walks with her mother.

Not exactly a rebel of Sacred Heart (this would be Kath), Nuala could motivate a rebel's grin, and Denny had earned his wink. The laundry line moved as one ensemble between the window outside the kitchen and the oak at the higher bank of the Dodder. Work shirts and towels, Denny's socks, Nuala's uni jumper, Kath's ol' Hello Shitty. They let the kettle boil furiously and in a crimson painted ceramic pot they had found in Portobello, Nuala allowed the tea to settle while Denny made cinnamon toast. They carried these onto the patio, where a few lavender columbines swayed in front of the green ivy. The yard air was musky from a cross-street neighbour's peat. It hadn't been particularly cool in the morning but the old man liked to keep warm and had grown up on one of the islands. Today, though, it was a small woodpecker who was trying to make room in Mr Waters' chimney; so he decided to send smoke signals using the best turf he had. He also liked nothing more than the smell. 'Maple, oak, saltwater and coffee! Maybe a little vanilla sprinkled in!' Denny imitated Mr Waters' accent. Apparently the Waters never made it to Virginia, nor to Massachusetts – but Ireland landed them, and to South Africa and Australia if they were lucky. The years of good cracking and fancy dancing were all in front, and behind, the old man. 'I'm nothing but a walker and a dream!' he'd say to Denny, the sun smiling through the gap in his two top teeth.

Chapter Twenty Eight

Clean-up day along the Dodder was coming near, and if it hadn't been for the rhino there'd be a lot more 'artefact' up around Denny's. Oak roots would be hangers for sundry carts and carriages. South along the Dodder, residents, dog-walkers and naturalists still had to pull out the odd bed-frame, petrol tanks, floating tyres, even a stove. Had a hurricane spilled into her? All the tiny brooks begat from the clouds above Wicklow added up and pulled their might. Even they didn't know what they could do together. Denny had volunteered for the River Action Committee, and he'd do it again in a quick second – not only due to the barbecue they all held afterwards but because he saw more than he ever would as he stepped no more than a couple feet at a time, for a quarter of a kilometre on the east side of the Dodder if it was sweltering, and on the west if he wanted the warmth. Of course, if the weather was crap it simply didn't matter: Denny deemed himself 'a real Indiana Jones' in the worst weather.

Two robins pecked around the rim of the grass near the oak and a coal-tit swayed on the laundry-line. The robins apparently wanted what the tit had but the tit had nothing but a free swing, a gentle lift and swing. You could almost hear the little bird giggle.

Kath had tried to tell Denny, years back, that he shouldn't ever wait for the Saint. 'The Saint waits for no one.' Denny was thick to see it. He was a valet to the Saint's charm, as he was an eternal novice at snooker. Now that the Saint was gone, he'd play the same music they used to listen to; louder or not at all, he thought. Maybe he'd even risk finding his own tunes, Kath hoped. Kath was sure to load plenty of what was current – or what was mad tasteful, sickly awesome. She knew her rock history and where punk had punked it; she was a product of the British invasion. You could put it that way. Some product. Nuala's would always be more catholic in comparison. Still, where Flogging Molly met the Drones, and where the Beatles, the Stones and U2 met DJ Upyrs, Nuala made room for them. 'An always-expanding liturgy,' Den', she'd say. Just like 'Ireland says Yes'.

Earlier in the week they'd received a letter – an actual letter – from Sarge. He was learning the dialects of Nigerian enlisted men and the cooks, having losing poker games with the Dutch contingent but enjoying the rub, and maybe – just maybe – falling in love with the food and the local temperature. He bypassed all the bad stuff, except to write that some of the officers were still living like class is everything and that the sight of the recently dead made him think he might become religious. Nuala noticed he'd folded the letter twice as many times as he needed to, as if to make the letter small and carried like a secret – or like the private wishes of someone who knew its value and wanted to be sure it reached its destination, like a strong cork for the message in the bottle. 'You go as long as you can go, until you can't,' Sarge had told them all, outside the leisure centre in Rathmines, before he turned to walk back to the barracks. They'd been talking about the Saint. What took him. Why he had to go. What's to be had in a life inside nineteen, twenty, twenty-one. And all else? Is every hour gravy – the phrase Denny's grandparents' always used – or can we not waste one moment thinking about every hour. 'Just live it!' Sarge added to the conversation earlier in the night, sounding a little frustrated. After all, Sarge was used to moving on. Yet here he was, from Nigeria, holding on to his friends by the tether of a deliberately folded letter.

Chapter Twenty Nine

'Who and where is G-O-D,' Denny asked the bleepin' sky.

A garbage truck was idling down the road. Generator for regeneration. Torque and belts of an elevator revved, spinning. But the sky would not lift.

The tech director sleeping in, Denny wanted to remark.

A janitor in the back of the stage flipped a few switches. The point, off at sea, showed; the mistaken bed-post tenting its vague longevity. The little window-shade of lighthouse started to provide something reachable.

The tide was so low, the waves came in like shadows. A seal resembled a swimmer and serpent by dips and bobs. A loon cleaned its feathers on top of a raft.

How do the loons fly into the density of this fog? Denny wanted to demand testily. Atmosphere and water appeared to be the same mass. They had agreed to a sequential trade in the artful dance of vapours.

'Vespers,' Denny spoke out loud. 'Where there can be no horizon.' The white horizon had folded into the white smears of fog and light upon fog on water, and there was no crease to be seen.

No one was saying Denny was different now. It was only that Denny felt the semi-constant mild insecurity of being without something, as if a blanket was taken away from a warm body sleeping in the cold. 'Live it,' Sarge says.

Someone – a guest from the neighbour's – was going fishing. Denny used to fish. With his Dad. He could fish again, for food; his philosophical position about the food-chain had changed to include forgiveness and protein. He could stomach what a person needed. He could even live with his own respect for other creatures and indulge in the occasional domesticity of animals. And crustaceans, the sacrificial birds: they were as human as they would be greens. In the years since Denny's childhood, whatever fishing he did was always catch-and-release. He'd watched fathers and sons along the Dodder before, and especially with Kath, when they'd sit along the canal, tired of having nothing to do.

The 6.55 flight resonated through the blinds. Hair-clippers gyrating from underneath. In relatively shallow water, a two-leg-thick fire-hose rippled its black mystery eight feet along the surface and disappeared.

What Denny couldn't see was a boat, and then another boat: a squadron of boats that must have set out well before first light. They seemed tangled in a braid, finding the same fish, as if they'd been dropped from the sky; the search parry was searching where the greys took on a resemblance to some normal reality, like onlookers – listening to someone busking, or rescuers standing vigil over a scene. Simply by the fact of their clustering, they made a contract with the hole in the weather.

Hard as it was to believe, amid ongoing wars and keeping up with business, people were enjoying holidays – all over the world. A man was chopping vegetables in the kitchen beyond the screened door of the bayside house he was renting. A family was dining on mussels and hen in wine country. Newly married twenty-four-year-olds were tentatively smiling at their server after a day of hiking or diving. Grandparents moored on their sailboat sat reading, and were about to Skype their grown children and grandchildren thousands of miles away.

Nuala wanted Denny to enjoy their life forming along the Dodder as if each day could be a holiday. And when the holidays came, they'd be ready: they'd know how to handle the pleasure.

'Every day a holiday, Den' – ' and then she kissed him on the cheek.

'And tell me which holdiays Michael will have, Nuala!'

She'd rarely seen Denny in such a forlorn mood. Kath had warned her. 'Your new man, Denny,' Kath told her – taking her aside the first time they'd met – 'he's not all aces and kings, you know.' Afraid Nuala thought Kath meant Denny wasn't as smart as he certainly was beneath the moss and mending, Kath added quickly: 'I mean, he can be emotional, you know? Lovely, but withdrawn sometimes – you know? I hope he won't go down that road with you but, um, I've seen him there and he just needs a rational pat on the broad side, y'know?'

'Oh, you've got me there, Den'. Maybe they have celebrations – days off – wherever he is.'

Denny just stared at Nuala, with a scowl that turned into a smirk. She had a way of leading Denny to laughter that was altogether different from Kath's. Without much effort, Denny found sympathy and acceptance of his selfish sensory habits. Nuala didn't ever know she'd be so effective in turning him around, but she certainly had a near-perfect record.

'Maybe the Saint's leading tours of smugglers' caves,' Nuala said, to break him of his mood.

'Or captaining a Segway Polo squad to the constant applause of his team,' said Denny, dryly, before snickering.

Chapter Thirty

What blooms in the eyes of boys dies in the hearts of men.

Denny was the epitome of youth, Nuala helping to make mature his morning-noon-and-night, as he hoped he did hers. Yet they could be playing grown-ups while the teenagers in them owned the moments. Just, the same sea played with borders, their bodies pushed limits they could not control. A scarf here, a sports cap there, shoes both older and new, Nuala and Denny were living 'old and young' in a neighbourhood where most people were entrenched in families, jobs, a monthly social obligation.

The huge hem of bay touched and tickled the shore, and both Denny and Nuala knew the feeling. A blue beach umbrella lifted its trim and let the air fill its insides. The white metal stem was something Denny knew, and when the arms of the umbrella appeared to stretch in a gust, the pole wanted to rise above bay, over the horizon, and glide with the gulls. One gull stayed beneath the pier, where it had found refuge in seaweed and Styrofoam drift. *It's come here to die*, Denny thought, and said to Nuala, though he didn't want to utter it. 'Or to rest,' Nuala added more softly.

The sea water ebbed in, in a big undulating-belly way, as if something lived there. *The Saint's missing this*, Denny wanted to say, but didn't. Instead he told Nuala that what the water was doing made him feel even more like the umbrella. Nuala smiled. She had such a genuine smile: 'easy as summer', Nuala would admit.

They passed a couple in their late twenties pushing two trams. They looked like the perfection of an ideal unit. The four seemed to be

117

laughing. The toddlers wanted to feed the seagulls. An ice-cream vendor parked his three-wheeled bike on the corner overlooking the park. A poster for an Ai Weiwei retrospective coming to IMMA stood out on the wall behind him, over his head and above his right shoulder. It was a black-and-white photograph of a woman in a short dress doing what looked like 'a Marilyn Monroe', as soldiers walked behind her without noticing. Denny noticed.

'The sacred "trinity" is blessed with good intentions – and attention,' Denny had teased Kath in earlier times, and Nuala had benefited from the tease when the days turned to springtime's anatomy.

If they were feeling old because of their place on the block, they were far from ever being accused of being 'spent'. To be young is the eternity the sea brings in.

And about the 'old things' the sea brings in? These, too, were new again. Pablo Neruda didn't beachcomb for old age. He sifted the shore for what made him feel new – nostalgia aside. No, if Denny was to become an old man, it would have to be with Nuala, and with Nuala there was no feeling aged.

They walked back to the mouth of the Dodder, to the locks, checked their watches and turned back home. 'What do you suppose Sarge is doing right now, Nulee?'

'Fighting off . . . *admirers*,' Nuala asserted. This would be good, considering Sarge's incomplete record of accomplishment back in Rathmines – much as his talk would have it otherwise.

Kath had sent a message they were receiving now as they approached their front door. 'Going to a movie,' the message said. 'Decide to join me or count your fates!'

After tea they'd go to the city centre and spend a few hours with Kath, like in the old days. Their favourite rap was playing, and Sarge and the Saint were almost there in spirit. By morning, the news of the world had changed, and everything could begin again. They would add a little to the discord, but it wouldn't be more discord. They'd head out the same as they always could and usually did, and count the distractions as mostly gifts – not biding their time, but riding it. Time and time again.

Chapter Thirty One

The birds were making music sounding like monkeys, and the bed-room-door handle chimed when Denny's bathrobe sleeve hit it. The 7.45 train oboe-ed through the valley, amplified by the hills.

Home is the memory of perfect mornings. Whether calm, serene, idling at the table or in a crisp outfit straight off the line, almost rushing to some pride at work, late August was the king on his pillow willingly preparing to de-throne. The neighbourhood appeared to turn its back on the mountain. The streets in rows made shy corridors, but this way the cars faced or returned from the mountain as its geological epicentre.

What was so special about the Saint is that he was special. Sarge had almost said as much at the October memorial. 'He had just started to live,' Sarge started to say, his long neck bent to the microphone inside the stone church that had been the Saint's parents' refuge twice a year during their marriage. It was here that the two parents had stood for their wedding, when maybe the Saint was a twinkle in their eyes. Doubtless he was there. His mom would say it's what brought them together, standing at the end of the aisle, saying 'I do' and 'I will'. The place was dark, and only yellow light illuminated scenes from Scripture, novelised on the six boats of stained-glass windows framed in mahogany. The altar was a pile of stones brought in from a bay. The roundness of them belied the angles the wedded, or the dead, would have to climb and negotiate throughout their lives – no matter how short or long those lives might be. Maybe the priests did this for a reason? To soothe the eyes from angles that would emerge. Why anticipate the corners? 'Keep it round,'

Denny could imagine hearing a priest say. Certainly baptisms were the exceptions – a time without angles. '"Keeping it round," cried Mary!' observed Kath, keeping it as Biblical as she could go. '"The feminine" in abundance. About time!' But the roundness of births and the bays of oceans have tensions and traumas too, omissions and seizures, years of pitfalls and years to round.

The round stones reminded Denny of bowls he and the Saint would use in their Rathmines flat. The Saint always ate quickly. He would spend a long time cooking (oatmeal or eggs in the morning, bacon or sausage, toast; Brussels sprouts with fennel, caramelised onion, cheese – and in the evening, as if to dispatch a revolution for one, fried Spam). Denny was the opposite. What was easy made him easily fed. He took an enormous amount of time with everything he ate – gyros, canned Tomato-Os, pizza, or nuts. By the time the Saint had washed, sponged, rinsed, dried his bowl and placed it in the communal rubber rack to the right of the tiny aluminium sink, Denny would just be beginning his meal. And off the Saint would go, to his room, to his music, to sleep, or into the night – and to where Denny didn't know. When Denny finished eating, the flat was quiet. The row-house next door, the one adding an extension – or a wall! – below Denny and the Saint's kitchen window, grew a shadow the way a man's face grows a beard. 'Never a family member, only the old man working; the mason, bent over cinder block swirling cement like a toddler in a mud puddle – dreamin', dreamin'! Can you imagine! To be old like that, working for someone else's benefit and for half a euro, dreamin'!' Sarge had said with more than a little scorn and absolutely no envy.

'Pity the old man?' Denny asked.

'Old people don't need any pity,' the Saint injected with authority when they were all staring out the window together one early evening, offering a pat homily: 'They just want you to quote a Beatle, mate.'

Denny and Sarge looked at one another, puzzled. 'All you need is love,' the Saint stated without singing.

Whenever Denny finished a meal at their 1970s red and silver speckled table next to the metal trash can with a step-release top, he saved his bowl after the merest of rinses and tucked it into a corner he had claimed during his first days in Lower Rathmines. Unlike the Saint, whose efficient manner suggested he'd never have need of one thing twice, Denny viewed his bowl as a thing he'd always need again. It was a noticeable difference between them. One would keep nothing and do everything. The other would save everything and have done nothing. In this way, Denny couldn't help but admire the Saint. 'He knows what to do; he doesn't falter.'

As they each took turns at the pulpit, they each touched the smooth round stone at one moment or another. Some, like Sarge, seemed to touch the rock unconsciously. Others smoothed it as if they were stroking the fur of a cat. Denny 'patted' one bulbous one protruding below his left hand, and it felt like the rump of a rhino. For Kath, the thing was like the maidenhead of a ship. She sort of gave it her blessing. It seemed the cold grain was a fascination and a reality-check, reacting to their hands. Inside their chests, between belly-gut and sternum, there was a sliver of a knife that was actually a fire, a kind of night-light that felt like a dangerous pilot, a shard of piercing flame that held heat like glass – sometimes 'melting' them until they curled over into it, like a freezing wave or a grown person retreating back into the foetal position. They were, in fact, 'still here', although the Saint was not. For Kath, it was as if the bay-stone had replaced the Saint. 'All down to this,' she spoke to the Saint's friends and relatives. She felt the weight of something in her throat and something in her eyes beginning to match the weight of stone. 'Love the dance,' she said, as if to say what the Saint would say; as if to declare him passed on in this life but not faded by the next. Nuala, the most piously educated of them all, began by declaring she didn't know 'what's next' – shocking, and somewhat pleasing, her friends with this ungirly atheism. 'But I know, as Kath knows, there's a suavey-legged dance in my future – and the Saint, bet you plenty, will be all over it.' Denny looked surprised. Had Nulee, too, been swayed by legacy made in mourning and a flash-drive of good looks in memory? Maybe the Saint's dying had shifted everyone – so nothing was more important, any more, than pursuing 'the next thing in front of you', as Kath insisted.

As for Denny, when it was his turn, he walked to the front of the church slowly. In the sixteen steps it took to reach the microphone, he felt the velvet of the ruby carpet and wanted to laugh. The Saint would have liked this, he realised – only he'd be in bare feet. The steps to the podium were like steps through early summer sand. All Denny could feel when he faced the people in the pews was the stillness of the air inside the church, a cave, yet daylight and the sense of themselves – strangers and friends – emanated, circulating. 'I want to say,' Denny began,

'Michael Saint Anthony was the best roommate I ever had.' [silence] 'He introduced me to music that matters most to me now – and will always matter, I'm sure of it.' [silence] There was more silence, and someone coughed several times. Denny still wasn't getting to it. He recounted the time the Saint and himself had visited the private club behind their flat, thinking they could kick a ball around the green. 'It was green, after all. We thought anything green was the universe's and should be shared. Of course we were also naive, and – I should add – without money beyond a small allowance, each. We were students, right? And we were good friends.' There was the holiday spent together at Saint Anthony's grandparents' farm, when they played basketball until midnight, laughing as if the stars were their brothers – and, oh my, sisters – two friends adding to the spectacle of the great solar system: dervishes driving to the hoop and the free-floating ball: three round things, swirling out of control but in bounds, one planet into another – and not a disaster.

The end leaves you wounded. No one to fuck you up. No one to curl to and cuddle. No conversation other than the mind's ear; an amber light on slowly falling snow. The Saint left his footprints where the earth is warmest, like the low mound of leaves around the roots of the maple tree: the ground, a familiar antique, an annual rust. Snow had come and gone and was descending again; the previously melted spots began to leap into the atmosphere once more as a thin veil put to rest; an imprint of what had been. With this, something ascends, if only the thought of it. 'Whys and hows and whens only make you a whysenhym'er,' forged Sarge. Sarge was upping his priority in friendship, he was on the call of duty, stunningly filling the need the quiet had left – like a good pacifist soldier. With Sarge's new role emerging, as if the Saint's bolt had hit Sarge in the pew – or feeling the rock, he was bringing Denny away from the whys and hows and whens into a sort of gratitude. This was a moment for acceptance no one had planned.

Out on the street, the wind was picking up and everyone's scarves were wrapping around their mouths and noses as if to prepare them for a spontaneous trek into the desert. Sarge laughed, which he did rarely. 'Lawrence of Araby!' he called. The reference stunned Denny and Nuala especially. Their laughter undid their scarves, and what was steamy for a few seconds felt suddenly cold again. The bell rang five and in the wind it sounded like guitar strings, or harpsichord. 'What that boy could do on the guitar!' said Kath.

'So swoon?' said Den.

'And Ba-ro-que again,' added Sarge, snidely, again surprising everyone.

'Jeeze, Sarge, we hardly knew ye!' ripped Kath.

The friends were back together. Minus one.

Tommy Keane seemed like an echo amplified faintly from a conch-shell as the gang of them walked into the breeze. The easy swirl of snow was miracle the Gulf Stream spun out of coarse seaweed and global warming. It was silver pence, 'hay pennies', flakes of fillings from the teeth of the recently deceased. And what moved in front of them was like the hand at Listons; dreamy characters reunited in the chalky dance deepening a blackboard, as if beneath it were a black whole full of happy masquerade: ah, frontier! The snooker balls were lined up and preserved for an unprovoked cue. The road, upon which sun declared its truths, redirected the abandonment of everything, and for this time all losses had gained a new direction.

Chapter Thirty Two

He dreamed by the tickling edge of the Dodder he'd be a Malta boy. He felt a bit girlish at the same time: grass at the place where you'd scream 'Ants!' – and hopefully never uncles. 'Girlish'? What is this anyway? Something Sarge would have teased? If Kath were any more girlish, she'd be a man. Maybe? It's like midnight: five minutes before and five minutes after. 'Two very different things.' Really? He didn't really have a take on what any of it meant. He knew what he liked, and this thing changed. 'No "ish", no "gir" . . . only "Irish".' Well, that too. He knew he knew something about the Dodder.

The inside of an envelope was the peeking edge of cool air on sunshine. He tried to imagine Nuala in the narrow hallway lined up with only slightly taller or shorter other young women, dressed in greeting uniforms for the incoming Sister 'of restraint and virtue'. Even at fifteen, Nuala had an inkling someone as refined as the visiting guest from the home convent must have had a life which involved another, a significant other, in addition to her God. This lady walked the path of students and shuttered the light that was hard as beams carved through the arched windows high above them. The younger ladies were arranged along this wall to the east of where the dignitary passed. As she stepped, she was motion itself developing the film. Strawberry-blond under curls tendrilled out from a loose bun. She walked with confidence, a brigade major between Europe and Africa, knowing that once the public display was over she'd sit with naked heels dug in to the cup-holder shapes in rugged coral, her tack and stirrup, at the underwater ridges of island, relief from municipal perception and a stiff position. Her power was her grace and also her adroit instincts to conceal.

Only twice had Nuala knelt with her class, next to their desks, while the teacher inspected every student's uniform-length. If the fabric rested on the floor, the pointer stayed relaxed in the sister's left hand. For those who ventured for whatever reason – a growth-spurt, a parent too busy or too encumbered to go out and buy a better fit, or even (forbid it) merely a bit of play – to display a quarter-inch's flesh, the blunt rubber nose of sister's pointer would slowly indicate where, what, needed to be covered. Many a nun was induced this way, and the habits of utility or fashion grew on some students more than others, but for almost all they began to feel their personal allegiances to God and various gods.

Kath was one who found 'God in the gods' as she insisted, rebelliously. Anyway, there were many paths to religiosity and knowledge. 'Punk was not born in eight days – but an instant of imagination helped,' Kath justified. 'Nor symphonies, rock and roll, hip-hop, slapdash next – ' she quickly listed.

'The blues,' added Denny. 'Folk and the blues.'

All music, they agreed. Like any prayer and every sleeve's fashion: exterior impressions and interior will was for the individual and time to create. Havoc was a four-letter word if you didn't 'c', Kath argued to Denny along the canal when he was down in the pants and piped up with pity. 'Then you *have o* good time, Denny! Feck the "c" if you can't ride it but "c" it if you can!' There were no barred barracks in Kath's quarters; she was the snarl of a tiger Denny needed – and at the time he needed most, only he wouldn't have thought so. He was a thin feather compared to the crew captain of the Rebels of Sacred Heart. Nuala had dated such a champion after taking her Leaving Certificate but he proved not to be a rebel in the ways of courtesy and understanding at all, but rather he saw himself immune to the necessity of those things. Nuala liked Kath because Kath could be a rebel while understanding those around her. Nuala had knowledge that allowed her the patience and respect she found in Denny. This was a matter of 'sacred heart' she probably wouldn't have acquired so quickly if she hadn't stood in the halls of parochial rigidity finding a glint and a clip of gait, an errant sprig in the light that could turn something difficult into softness, a representation of something 'other', even in the gaze and style of a conscripted life. She was reverent from the time she was held close to her mum, and the chores around her parents' house were easy if frequent. She glanced not a bad eye on anyone. This was her gift more than her fault. At the same time she could sense a cat's sharp claws before they were drawn and backed away with calm, speaking of people who slinked like cats. She knew a hole in the rug before she stepped on the spot; she could smell whiskey – the 'water of life' (my arse) – on the altar of a dysfunctional church before she stood at the front doors. She could lift Denny with the phrase of her eyes and this was usually all they ever needed, walking along the Dodder, in the city centre, or away on winged holiday.

Cloth was good if heavy in the early fall into late spring. Pierce's muted striped picnic blankets could double as bedding's wool. Nuala and Denny fashioned home from simple things: a lantern that had been Nuala's grandfather's, a cheese-box for bedside books, a deck-hand's trunk that never made it on to the *Titanic*, which they set in their living room to hold a vase containing what a hand would grasp from either the Dodder's banks or from vendors north of the urban centre near Jervis. There is no leisure in this life that doesn't take its happiness in found things. Denny had feelings about the castaways when he passed the charity shops in Rathmines. Perhaps he, for no right reason, felt himself a castaway. But so had Kath, at a time. So had Sarge. So had each of them. 'Even the Saint,' Denny admitted. '*Even the Saint.*'

They could objectify the object to make it figurative, but they refrained from objectifying the figure to cast one as an object only. Objects of imagination, though, were for inventors, reachers who finally find, collectors who offer another look, the writers and painters and sculptors and actors and dancers and composers and performers who risked the edge and fanned the floor in an unfancy flame; the fruits in the fork, by pull and climb. Instinct was a spring and a lever and what Kath, Sarge, Nuala and the Saint had learned at sixteen, seventeen, Denny was comprehending beyond eighteen – beyond anything, he'd look for springs and levers as long as he felt young.

Yeah, they'd gone to the charity shops to spring themselves up. Too long in the dank and they needed a new perfume.

Skirts up, surf's up,
       a fiddlehead in the snow.

A bunch of daisies under these,
       & moss before the peat.

Bring on the sea &
       turn up the heat.

Sarge sang the words like there was no distance, no difference, between the teenage Sarge, remote and reclusive in Finglas, except for a good rap and adolescent craic – to bust out of his many shades of brick-house blues. The charity shops had this gift. For hardly anything, you could be King again. And if you were a girl: this was your billion-dollar photo shoot to stardom – in an instant.

'Sometimes it feels good to get into someone else's clothes,' says Nuala, shopping with Kath. This surprised Kath, a bit. Seeing Nuala relaxed did the same for her own mood. Suddenly the cold touch of the satin lining in the arms of the tunic she was trying on tickled her enough to cause her to smile and squeal like she'd just put her foot in a bucket of ice-water. Sarge was lost in the hat department, posing in the corner like a slugger.

Kath breathed in and exhaled, pleased with all of their options: 'The road to fashion wasn't styled by only one person's tastes alone, was it Nulee?'

They each tried on someone else's cotton blouse, then shoes. Heels where heels had never been. It was a sanctified adultery, a clean commissioned crime, a shag in socks in a whole shop, potentially, of onlookers; mirror and glass to the street – and the smiles on Nulee and Kath's faces suggested they'd just gone somewhere where no girl by either of their names had ever gone, at least in this store at that hour and on the date illuminated on their phones.

Nulee got the clogs and Kath purchased the retro top and they both sprung out into evaporating moist air that suggested warmer days and fewer clothes ahead. The weather felt like end-of-school days, nights lengthened from leisure into further leisure a person could almost call hedonistic – except they were only 'kids', still, by standards of the working middle class, and certainly by the less visible leash their parents tried to tug around holidays and 'Have we a job, now – have we?'

This was time for Kath and Nuala to stretch their feet.

At the leisure centre one side had a row of arcade games. The sounds were foreign but tantalising. A circus parade in Casablanca, maybe. A black-light dance club in the shoddy Fillmore. An Italian ice truck lit up and sounding its carnival music on a flat-bed ferry to Innisfree. An invitation to alien pageantries. Once, Denny had walked through the section as though he were passing the come-ons of drug dealers and prostitutes. 'Lollipops, half-quid for two dozen,' they could have been pushing in his ears. The fronds of velveteen and leather, cotton-candy perfume and greasy floorboard aftershaves, 'Feck This' T-shirts and florescent knee-highs, caution orange eyelid gloss, teal-grey lipstick and bearing-encrusted cheek-spikes. The list was unimaginable but like anemones the sea gives birth to multi-fad brains and eyes with a lurk for arresting hormones and empty aesophagi associated with adolescent hunger – and all are not lost but keep watch. It felt like a long time since he'd been inside the leisure centre with Sarge, or the Saint, or by himself. It was an aeon since he met Kath next to the pool table in the corner they frequented in front of the cashier's booth: 'Any friend of Sarge is a friend of mine,' Denny had been willing to accept back then, fuelled by the social activity he felt he should join – or else be daft. The heavens had sheltered him in Kath's streetwise go-it-easy. He didn't have himself to thank. Supposing the barbershop music joint wasn't around, he would not have been exposed to new music except what he overheard on the Grif' 15. He'd arrived like an orphan and looked like a squatter without a quill. Fifteen hundred euro was supposed to get him through his first nine months in Dublin. He figured he'd listen to the radio, but the flat didn't even have that. The Saint had brought the soccer ball they rarely used. Other than the faded plaid couch and a kitchen window, there was no entertainment console, so to speak. The smallest available Alstar Cooke electric 'fireplace' – they called 'the rotisserie' – was the single cheap gimmicky exception. But every time Denny walked past Listons it was the chalkboard that told him something about the future he needed to know. It wasn't all Annie Bee Summers, but some of it was. After all, he was a boy in a country of men: O'Brien, O'Connell, O help me, O my – and if cable-knit didn't suit him or was passé, terebinth in the nostrils did; pine slouch from ulterior landscapes; flash charity maxi on a cosmopolitan min; a game in the rush of trickle-down, from the ceiling to Wicklow to what Denny's toes felt eventually in the curve-flow of the Dodder. Nothing Ballsbridge or the wide eye of the US embassy could move would harness as much sympathy as this spot of water. Unannounced, just as Listons' hand, the scrawl became language, became age, became him in the guise of a growing young man. Sarge would do it in the army. The Saint, any way he could – and did, sleeplessly and with a pity that was actually pretty to the blokes and ladies who wanted to know him as their teammate, brother, dance-partner, friend and lover. O'Africa, for Sarge. O'Regularity for Kath. O'Companionship for Nuala. O'What for Den. O'Death for Saints.

Chapter Thirty Three

He could not be angry towards him the way he could if the Saint had been a suicide. It would have been easy to say to himself 'forget all this, he had his chance' and toss every remembrance of the Saint to the deep-six drawer of No More. Worse than underground, above which one gets rightly sentimental, and if any forgiveness was necessary it will kick in, it would be as if a suicide never existed – not the death of it, not the life of the one who could have survived. In a lot of ways, Denny wished he could have never forgiven the Saint for having gone. But there was nothing uproarious about the Saint's leaving. If Denny felt mad, there was Nuala to bring him back to their imaginary prairie homestead, horizon, pipes and whistles. Kath was the one less likely to sit in that dark and soggy cell of misbegottens but if ever she was, Denny was the friend to hand her the earplugs, touch the music library they'd made together years back, sit back on the bench with her near Sandymount and wait seven seconds for her to grin. Tears would line her face like a happy prisoner behind two bars, her smile pushing the liquid iron further and further away. Sarge brooded in the way only a soldier can. He showed affectionately little emotion, made himself scarcer and scarcer, but focused himself headlong into projects he would not have volunteered for in the old days. Such as duty in Nigeria.

Whenever Sarge and Denny had acted like immature young men, Kath called them on it. 'The problem with old men is that they were young men!'

'Wha'ja mean?' Sarge demanded.

130

Denny knew what she was getting at. Even as boys mature, there is an elemental immaturity about them. 'It's just the nature of men.'

Denny didn't believe all boys had to turn out to be older boys who were stupid. He didn't think that young men necessarily treated women with indifference or as objects. 'There are plenty of examples of males being good, thoughtful and kind,' Denny wanted to interject into the conversation, but he accepted that this wasn't a conversation so much as it was Kath 'letting them know'. She had a sisterly quality about her in this way. 'She keeps you on your toes,' Sarge said more than once.

And so usually Kath knocked Denny out of his doldrums, her own brand of smelling salts at hand. 'Look at you! Look at you!' she could say with venom and love in the same snarl.

Denny looked at himself – the self he could see from inside himself, at least – and he saw that he was still here – and with Kath, at that. That he was OK was a long way from where the Saint was now. Even if the Saint *was* OK, wherever he is.

'Feck a bear, Denny, feck a bear!'

And she was correct, as usual. Sometimes it was love and sometimes it was poison but to wake one out of forever-evers one had to go deeply into the knells to feel oneself again and to feel 'the glories of being alive', as the priests would say.

Chapter Thirty Four

What like this can you do in death? It was a solitary thought commenting on nothing Denny could particularly avoid. The mysterious 'something' hidden in the commentary was what he had known probably ever since he was a boy, even since conception. He wondered if Kath and Nuala could think such things. He hoped they would. Would a girl? He hoped they did. If they didn't, he was going to feel awfully alone. The rhino could feel these things, he was sure of it: all those 'ladies' hiding in the sheets of valleys after the spring flowers had made a fence for finding, a crib for a secret picnic, a sunning of themselves bare and barely, in the banks of the big 'v', as warmer weather made the river glint more, hot like sweat, contrasted by the drips of sweet tea. In fact, in the drought the rhino stood stronger, taller, with its pedestal revealed: what hunk, hulk, the nighttime student maids of mill towns circumvented until a sustained torque of August heat finally infuriated them, like a mad itch to go shopping and splurge on reckless things larger in price than they themselves could handle without guilt the next day, but in doing so, it was at last an unabashed stride into freedom before school. Denny felt he didn't even need to bet on whether or not Kath needed what he needed: some reassurance from love of nature, the let-go of the canal come March, a kaleidoscope of sun-rays behind a pair of smiling eyelids as salty waves made heavier sand where abundance was soaking; just shy of conception. Surely if we were habitual then a fond memory, like the face looking upward to shooting stars, would remember some colourful flush and eternity roiled together in the present in

132

wall-less light, through sheets a person could put hands through, a sat-iny, blanched mud sucking the depths to make longer time; a frequency for return journeys.

Nuala, he knew, stepped into the thick of day and time as a soldier in boots. Her growing up had made her satisfied only with what she did not have, and so she went for life's ephemeral mysteries as soon as she was twenty. The stained glass of ruby rosary and a forbidden medicinal blue, like the stinging strobes of Garda cars, still let light in, and it was pure: a white pulse that skirted the lead in the windows and over the warm hoods connected to headlights – the dark rubber bumpers thicker at two points to be sure – and the preventable calmed next to the Liffey, where two lovers imitated statues released from their frieze in gauze and cotton this time, like a spontaneous Halloween. To the eye, she was still in step-pers, but she'd given slack beneath the cable-knit only an altar boy with a peek to perception may satisfy in the lifelong dream of pursuing a new language. What do we call? How did you say? The tongue found way even on top of granite. The tongue made its own pronouncements on top and below the fabric that kept language in. Language seeped in like a need for realisation, a clarification of place and future, and Nuala – socks on or off – saw in the eyes of Denny civilisations that opened the books of present time to something joyful and endless she had always felt she claimed. Kath was there as a teenager, grabbing the reins, bridal and horse between four fingers, and spouting a mouth that was unforgiving until it was spent and puffy – like an argument that required no more air.

Chapter Thirty Five

Denny would wait until a sign from the universe withdrew the iron gates that seemed to leave him immature. How he admired the Saint's manhood even in boyhood. Even Sarge could not have been a boy's boy, although his neighborhood dictated he needed to act tough while he was as young as two. He'd slug around profanely by six, worse by eight, a hellion by ten. The dirty mouth then was a badge of honour, yes, but more than this it was the beginnings of a holster. Of *course* he sought refuge in the barracks. The barracks, for Sarge, were the difference between home and not home – which is to say, home could only be the barracks. If Sarge went back to where he grew up, he wouldn't be here. Nah, the holster would find itself at his side, where it should be, or under the arm, but he'd never be the live ammo like he felt he was in his parents' flat.

The Saint's lean body made him appear older than his youth could otherwise express. Twenty-five-year-olds were attracted to him when he was seventeen. He had the grace of a salesman's smile, which melted butter in the bowl like a marksman. To say grown women looked only twice when he got on 'r off a bus is to cheat them of all their individual idle moments. Something potent needed to be popped: an ice-water pool on the hottest day breaking the held breath into full breathing once the swimmer surfaced. What sizzled was to fry until it was lifted. The cool air, by contrast, rose a person's consciousness as if it were a budded sprig to the branch. Leaf and berry would have a go. Deer would come sniff, nibble and bite. The tree would bounce back after the spring of having been sampled.

Chapter Thirty Six

Nuala worked late on Fridays and she met Denny, sometimes, at the top of O'Connell Street for a film. They'd walk past the deceased poets and lawmakers, shadows in the huge glass fronts of ladies' stores and gentlemen's gadgets. The fluorescent prick measuring the always-standing RPMs between the GPO and the mod mere garments of summers – Gerty's shy and shyer bloom – where wars and the lingo flew, finally to provide a legal ledger in domestic commerce. They paused at a bronze of manuscript paper on a round, also bronzed table, a bronze pen exposing itself, adhering to the top. They touched the cool and smooth paper and Denny tried to pick up the pen. A bit of his own. The whole thing stood in a boat, big enough only for two – or three – beneath and around the one-legged table. It was pointed toward the mouth of the Liffey but Denny figured it could go anywhere from this point: the Indian Ocean, round the Horn, into the harbour where the Pilgrims picked up their messes and began to make their little prides. The ladies' stores were closing and Clerys middle managers were funnelling out like parliamentarians on leave; the café was being cleaned and in the city centre pubs and clubs were starting to spin, Scandinavian techno and Japanese hip-hop. Rathmines was only a little louder than it would have been most weekday nights; the charity shops had closed, leaving only traces of brown cardboard and a receipt. The windows of the prudently painted homes along the Dodder were largely vacant due to back-room suppers and or escapes to a second home, midlife crises or the early sleep of upper-age middle professionals. It was nearly a holiday, a sales clerk's

135

excuse for fun, and a teacher's free lunch; some could taste it, especially in Temple Bar, and increasingly around the Needle.

Nuala undid the top button of her white blouse and Denny took off his hat. Seagulls laughed at what craic a passerby would relent to give, and she scampered to lift the morsel to her frayed feathered gullet. A Nigerian man sold watches near where Denny sometimes caught a bus and Denny instantly visualised Sarge. He wished he'd written a letter to him. Nuala hummed a tune Denny had never heard. Its melody, at first, was like a song Denny heard out west – or a Linton Johnson tune. *Tune* was hardly correct. More like *drumbeat*. 'Bass double down', a reggae story. There was melody enough after the rhythm came. Of course it was music but only an old person would have called it a tune. Even in an elevator it wouldn't be a 'tuuuuune'. Nuala said it was a pop song and, sure enough, she was giving him the elevator version. 'All the way to the 'nth floor, OK?' Denny requested. Nuala kept humming. At the same time Nuala wondered about Kath; what was Kath doing this night? She would have hated the movie. Not one lesbian and barely a bisexual!

'The narrator is trans,' Denny stated, firmly.

'Oh, I see . . . ' Nuala said. 'Yes, transforming literature. Kath would have preferred the book.'

'Indeed,' said Denny. 'Me too.'

'Me three,' chimed Nuala between hums.

'Kath would have approved of the movie,' Denny reappraised, 'if only the man had been a woman.'

Nuala scowled. Back to the game, they were: 'Me all of me three,' she added, taking a breath before the next hum.

'Sure enough,' exhaled Denny. 'Buy the book!' He imitated in Kath's voice. 'Or see the film and be glad,' Denny resolved.

A night out was like making a world. You could be undersea divers or explorers into the future and no one would have the foggiest idea what you were up to or where you were. Your parents would be on the phone or in a Lay-Z-Boy watching the news and not doing a diddly thing about it. You could call them any time from anywhere in the universe and they'd be right there, sitting, chewing maybe, or glad they had two lips and a tongue, even if it was only opening and closing, like fish, to breathe air.

The Saint's film-days were over, although the fathers said he would be seeing all the films he wanted in his majesty's heights. 'Ah, shoestrings and knickers!' Kath would say, pretending to sneeze. 'There ain't nothing the living can do to save their souls' – Kath would then pause dramatically – 'except sneeze and run! Tie your shoes tight and slip 'em off at night! Sneeze and run, sneeze and run; it's at least half the fun you'll ever have!' One thing Denny liked about Kath was that no matter how cynical she could become, she always had room – secret silly sultry room, as it happened – to lighten up a dour place. 'May the Saints light your knickers for some but not for your mum to see' was Kath's parting advice to Denny after they'd relaxed from being more-than-friends. Their days were numbered as soon as they met but fortunately their numbers kept going up. They could be friends, and – what's better – Nuala and Kath could be pals as well. 'Denny in the middle!' Ah, Denny in the middle. Denny always felt in the middle, or else left out. It was OK. After the mountainous heights of holding the baby jayzus in the holiday play when he was not yet five years old, a blue blazer and a tie and already a thing for Mary – who was right next to him, her embroidered flower on the puffy short sleeve of her white dress touching his own cotton shoulder sounding like sandpaper on wood to his ear. He knew what *like* was, but he didn't know what *love* was. Thank the depths for Kath. She could see a blind cat under a garbage lid in a dank alley she had a song to sing about. 'Denny, Denny, Den', Den'!' she'd rapid-fire from her quick slick tongue as though she were her own snare. Nuala ought to thank her every day. Imagine the mess he'd be in if not for her rescuing him.

Chapter Thirty Seven

On the weekend, Nuala and Denny drove the motorway, the inland 'gateway', as it was called, and then bucked off and took minor roads through towns they never knew existed, even though Nuala ought to have remembered, to get the happy and lost way, supposing, to Sligo. Denny'd been to Sligo a couple of years before with the Saint and Kath, sniffing out where the big literati lived – like sleuthing the trail of Harry Potter and what's-her-name – the young actress Denny wanted to fall in love with. They were practically giggly about it. The village seemed mere layers of shadows. Since they were dependent on the bus-schedule and their wits during that first trek, they rather missed the big town itself, whatever it might have kept for them; secrets to be kept and realised when they came back. The bus was a log in the brown river of town. Denny thought he'd return, as the hulk banked the curve as if to underline a frown. He thought he saw a bookshop (gone!), and a Chinese restaurant (gone!), and a dry-cleaner's (gone! – but the vision lingered; something about stiff white sheets, silky buttons, fresh and square).

'Someday I'll be man enough to press my shirts – I mean to have them pressed,' he hoped.

Nothing about town back then said convincingly *stay*, but they could hear the whispering of the ocean, although it was too late for them – on the bus as they already were. Mick was with them in cowboy style but he turned mighty sad, dreadful-looking, to be on the bus. He avoided buses the way wild horses avoided pavement. Cooped up like that. He looked like a hunt dog in a cage while all along he'd been told he'd be chasing ducks. Mick lowered his cap and began to snore. Anything to avoid actual confinement. He'd wake up in Dublin or Galway, a dream. A Galway handy girl or a German seamstress. Which ones, it didn't matter. Mick could be a cowboy wherever he landed – city, suburb or country – just never put him on a bus. Even if they'd wanted to hitch, they could no longer do so legally along the managed carriageways. The stories of meandering travel from the backpackers of yore – some of it was gone. However, if you had friends on one side or the other, though not as fast as a plane, the M-digits would carry you by coach faster than your average pre-boarding wait in an airport would take – accepting security, of course. The country was like a narrow waistband now, and instead of beatin' about the bush in a parochial way, a person could be driven from one end to the other almost as fast as a tongue on ice.

Instead of the straight shot, this time away from the M-s, Nuala led Denny the way she'd remembered – only many of the places felt new to her, as though she were passing through her parents' dreams, not her own, only she was definitely in it, she was the real McCoy, she was prime and pride and sure . . . she was in the driver's seat. She drove like she was sewing a skirt, readjusting the car smoothly as lane bent into lane, circles replacing intersections, and handling curves with the patience of a raft gently propelled by a wake, only to slow to a stop in a full breath held there like she was poised to sing or answer a nun's ultimate question with an acceptable answer. Denny sat back admiring her efficiency – and felt a little out of control because of it. He was not one to adhere to sequences. He thought he had affinity for the gaps. Still and all, he was actually kind of turned on by the way Nuala navigated, and the fact that her knees were nearly constantly moving to facilitate the shifting. He'd wished he'd gone to school with her, and he wished, thinking better of his current position, he didn't. Like when he called her parents' house. Nope! No way, son! Have your own cracker over tea. All of Denny's pious upbringing, singing in the chorus, the good kid mowing the lawns: 'All of that and a can of worms still doesn't appease a parent!' Denny knew from her father's first in-your-face kind of rushing to the phone '*Hell*-o!' that he was lucky never to have been the lad from the boy's school, angels all forbidding.

Into a valley they saw an industrial town where there was a field at the edge near a school. Between the school and a dairy farm, Fossett's Circus had set down their blue-and-orange-striped array of tents and caravans. Denny felt ten again, and then fifteen. The bareback rider, he remembered.

'Appropriately named,' he decided on the spot. 'Mona!' he heard Kath's imaginary voice suggest to him as Nuala drove like silk through linen eyes past the cars and people lining up. So often Kath's voice seemed the voice of Denny's conscience. He'd accepted her superior intuition and intuited her imagined responses inside his own, while his own mind made itself up. In Nuala, it was her gift of perception he admired.

They got to Strandhill just in time, before the last surfers had called it a day, before afternoon was too late and had to be evening. The sand was cool to their soles, barefoot. Their feet felt like their palms, tender and prepared. A few rocks startled their feet and their toes gripped for a soft edge, their soles sucked upward like an umbrella or a mollusc responding to predators. Denny thought about the journalists who'd had their soles tortured while they were captive in places where conscience was just a tool. They could let the shore do the speaking for them, and their direction had no pre-planned choreography. As Denny went right, following the bubbled 'lines' of the ocean's trailing, Nuala went left and appeared to focus on individual stones. They met together somewhere around the knees, the north Atlantic a wash around them underneath where they could no longer see for sure, and salt ringing its translucent garters around their lower thighs. Denny stood there, a more mature sapling, a couple of branches and an ordinary crown reaching the clouds now. Unable to get a word out – except 'C,' 'C!,' as if his body was interpreting *sea* as the sound it made only in the character of the curled letter 'C' – for the arched curving serif of ocean wave fastening a rider in its middle, like a buckle, a fitting in that lovers could know once they knew it.

Barbecued prawns woke him as they wafted from the Strand Restaurant stand, and even though Dubliners were told their bay prawns were the best, these surprisingly more pungent Sligo sliders suggested a kick Denny thought must be at least three-quarters Cajun, and basil and thyme. 'Szechuan cooking's a big thing here, Den',' Nuala said. She could tell he was still trying to identify the flavours. 'More than one town in every county has made a rock-star out of a Szechuan Shamrock – usually courtesy of "the mainland", or else busier places in the EU!' She'd been here with her cousins twice just for the food (and for a hen party the next day; a friend from home was about to be the first to put her finger in the sluice).

The aroma, street fair and summer, sent Denny daydreaming about America. As a family, holidays were enjoyed at home, in the backyard, or – if the parents had the time – to a camp. 'Little out of pocket and some change to bring home' was Denny's father's modus operandi. It was quite enough that fuel prices continued to rise. The problems parents had were of no interest to Denny or his friends except when their plans were to be derailed by adults. 'You're not the only cup in the cupboard,' Denny's gran would tell him – although it never made sense to him: a person *chooses* to use a cup or doesn't, and the cup doesn't have a say in the matter. It meant, he supposed, that every cup had to be washed and dried, not just the one. And washing required the attention of a responsible person. The love of grandparents, and parents, didn't have to be artificial, but it was a love of differences too: different times, different preferences, different style, different rules and obligations. Respect usually fused. It wasn't out of unkindness or selfishness that Kath also made a bolt for a life that excluded her own family at the time. She was ready by the age of three and she had the jones to be grown up by eight. So by twenty, she'd begun making a life for herself that was the envy of her parents, her aunts and uncles, her classmates who wanted to be her – except without the rough part.

'Dublin prawns for your sorrows!' Kath had brought a bowl of them one Thanksgiving to Denny's and the Saint's in Rathmines when the rain never let up. The Dublin variety had been sprinkled with ginger and pepper and something that tasted a whole lot like sugar and sea salt. Enough to make a young man sit up straight.

'And prawns in your boots!' Denny shot back.

They'd only ever shared one Thanksgiving. One was enough. If you're thankful once in your life, you might as well be thankful for the whole thing. The opportunity doesn't necessarily fade. Denny was thankful Kath wasn't a preacher, but she sure could pretend to her friends.

The smoke from the Strand created little moons which gave rise to Denny thinking about Five Lamps, the memorial back in Dublin, at North Strand – more like a candelabra for nineteenth-century vehicles, a sort of elaborate street-light so drivers didn't collide at the intersection, Sarge had noted when they were all there. Kath had taken Denny, the Saint and Sarge to see the spot, perhaps in an effort to sway Sarge into thinking he could try for his certificate and leave the army. 'Munitions were for mortars,' she'd tell him, slurring 'mortars' to sound like 'murders'. 'And I bet you didn't think Dublin was bombed during World War II, did you?' she said, pointedly staring at the Yank, and Sarge as well.

Sarge knew something about it, all right. He'd seen a military-history blog, he said, with crack-ignorant posts about how all Irish must be anti-this or pro- that because '*They* even liked the German soldiers.' Not true, and true. The Nazis bombed North Strand, and this is why we have Five lamps, Sarge explained. Of course it is also true that soldiers – no matter which tribe – were buried in a lovely country grave near Wicklow.

'Germans are people too,' Denny said.

'Have you ever been to Berlin?' asked Kath. 'Feckin' grand place!' she declared. 'If you want to dance, you should go to Berlin, I'm telling yous. The clubs are *fan-freakin'-tastic!* But let me tell you, it's not *because of* the bombing that we have Five Lamps. It's *because* Five Lamps remained that we remember the bombing!' Kath wanted to be sure to drive the point home. 'Before that, you'd be giving water in five directions for the people here. And now what? These motorists don't even know! Ah, how lovely: a *street-lamp*! If they even notice. Maybe it'll stop a car from bombing through the city. Maybe all it says, finally, is: Slow Down.'

'Maybe it's a lit stick up its arse and the architect of the Needle copied it!' mocked Sarge. A man of few words, but piercing.

Denny considered the souls of the German soldiers – in Wicklow and elsewhere – the Irish and the British, the Normans and the ones before, since, and in between, in the soil that filtered the rains that supplied the Dodder. He pursed his lips for Saint Patrick, too, and for Jonathan Swift, and for each of the little beehive people pushed out onto the Dingle peninsula like the horses were bearing down on them with the Iron Age and pointed helmets. He gave a thought to all the people who'd ever lived on the edge, in Soweto, in pueblos and worse. The bridges of America had seen plenty of needy after the gates of Ellis Island. But for the grates of New York City a person could be thankful for the heat. A pedestal could be a solid wall even if it was only three-quarters solid, against the forgiving bank of earth.

Chapter Thirty Eight

The ferris wheel at the port in Dublin was as close as he and the Saint ever got to living it up in the right old town, brother to brother. Even then, they chose to sit on a bench and talk about the girls walking by. (Would that it would be her highnesses up on the wheel, the flowing river underneath; the Saint's and Denny's eyes reflected, spots of diamond lights to the young women.) Denny had been to a place in the States, a suburban, smaller-scaled Coney Island, at Old Orchard Beach, when his family holidayed there a few times. Strandhill brought it back now. Alone, although alone with Nuala, maybe for the first time he felt he owned his space in the world. When he was with his family on vacation, the little carnival at Old Orchard Beach didn't have a 'Hall of Freaks and Wonders', only awkward families themselves and their villages of plasticised fake-wood caravans. But there didn't seem to be any popcorn and lobster at Strandhill, and while there were accents, they weren't from Maine or Canada. He heard South Africans, Scots, Danes, French, Germans, Chinese and Japanese, Brazilians, Australians, Kiwis, and of course Irish. And the Yanks. Of course, over the clink-clank of cutlery, there were the sounds of Yanks. By this point Denny could hardly hear them, though. In his ears it was only and all waves, shore, breeze, Irish and Nuala. In the waves were *bodhrán*, harp and uilleann sounds. In the air was tin-whistling, lilts and cracks. On land – boggy though it was – were two people as solid as they come. This is where the dance-hall started. Body electric, yes; a yes to Mr Whitman.

'To Nigeria!' toasted Denny.

'To all the Ns and Ms and alphabets in between,' added Nuala in a kind-hearted roast.

'To living.'

The breezes took it away as soon as the words were spoken but Nuala hoped someone might be hearing it along the beaches of South Africa, Cape Breton, Anaheim, Normandy, Goa, Isla Negra, every space where there are ears open enough to hear. Some say in a shell or in a bottle. Some say in the words themselves. Some say in *themselves*.

Whatever shame it was that Kath and Sarge and Mick and the Saint and the others who'd mattered in their lives couldn't enjoy this moment was not at all the point. The point was: the enjoyment was the point. And, out of respect, they wouldn't be there if not for them – 'them others', they'd say. 'Them others' were them, themselves included. No stiff at the bottom of a cold-cold monastic stone but the stirring creatures of imagination. To Mister Crapper and the ol' 814, to the horns up along the Dodder, to the slickened board near Sligo, bobbing cork – flounce on a bed of hard shed salt, to the distance between Lower Rathmines and northside watering holes 'where the thespians straighten the tongues of lesbian engineers' in mutual pride and benign shenanigans (leave it to Sarge to say . . .), in a land making comradery out of loneliness and music out of mud, fire from what was wet now dried to flame again our blue human history – craic and brawl, ball and spit, swagger and wager, tuck an' curl, fester and foam, grit and teeth, breath and syllable, underarm and behind the knee, loves frustratingly unpenetrable but slip-stream-brilliant by calculation or surprise: the novel expectation born of sitting slather and brine. Upended, like the bad news in yesterday's news-papers – letters' coal cuneiform, from blotch to smoke and smoulder and blotch again; into the soiled sky of never-end, into twang and twist of the individual instance insisting itself on a sheet.

In past times the news would have been fit for fish: fried, chips galore, a hefty shaking of salt, add your vinegar – light, medium or heavy (explain to a stranger it's tonic to your heart). Now for Denny it was popcorn in a bag made from newspapers rescued from a train station in Delhi. Some fleet of children, sent by an NGO, collecting the clean waste of the world – the fleeing public, out of time for work, remaindering it – repurposed in Denny's hands as the same water in another ocean soothed his cranium with its universal song. When he'd finished, he turned the bag over and read what he found. As if placed there, squarely at bottom centre, in 'the underneath', the so-called Sacred Space. 'Utterly Devoted', it said, though to say 'said' implies voices (and why not?). 'Having made thy Sacred Heart, thy Goal will grace thee.' It was confusing as much as fortuitously wanted. If there was a popcorn trick, this was it – maybe. No fleshy surprise, no fortune or lucky numbers; only seeds, kernels, these words. Flesh itself and the wind off the coast, the flow of time and the raised cup, the sentience of taking a stand. A little vinegar, salt, and words to carry out.

Chapter Thirty Nine

His jacket was falling apart – an animal shedding parts of its skin, leaving patches where smooth leather had been, was now a moleskin suede, the first fur of a baby rodent. But it was *waking* that was such trouble. He himself had been a golden child until, in a strip-mall, Santa Claus told him what Abraham Lincoln and John F. Kennedy had in common – besides being presidents. Waking was problematic, like an anaemic searching the dust for a nail. *Grain exports, Ukraine, the minimum wage in Germany, the firing of the French Minister of Economics in favour of a venture capitalist.* He wished he had used his phone instead of the leftover radio from the 80s to wake him up. *Maybe enough news is simply 'waking up',* he thought to the silence of his own cranium, which echoed with the lack of spectators in the bleachers.

The sun rising down the block and around the corner as the overworked auto-mechanic steps through reluctance again and again was enough of a daily occurrence to make Denny wonder why anyone would set their own alarm. He could feel the tiredness on other people; the narrowed sun checking a shoulder, like a tap – not necessarily a good tap either. A woman's head – mother or florist's assistant – hung as she walked, a weighted poppy in late season. Bronzed globe assembled from child's clay, cauliflower filled with dust and then overcooked. A chambermaid on her day off. The schoolkids were emerging in their chequers and straights, pushed out onto the streets like toddlers towards the swings. They bounced back from the day before as rubber balls, unsure of their purpose, but it didn't matter long, as they could count on the rubber and the wall. Their guardian's fatigue wore off on them like spit in the rain.

Denny tried to sleep for another five minutes. 'It makes you sad. Such a grim place to have to step into, first thing in the morning.' It was the voice of no one present. It seemed to be the voice of history keeping watch, or of the reluctant future.

The Saint didn't have trouble – he was up in a flash. He *was* the flash. Thing was, it was fool's flash, rainstorm on a bright yellow slicker – dry by noon. By midmorning he'd be fast asleep, the teacher's sonorous voice milking his dreams where the teats of cultural anthropology wandered back to leprechauns and silkies. Did the teacher notice? No. Perfect attendance!

'What you need, Den', is some swagger,' Kath said, to pump him up. While the others in his class were going out to the Radio Club, or whatever, Denny was watching the shopkeeps close up and go home: rags on mop-posts, cinderblocks for shoes, the whiff of whiskey or dishwash in their face. 'Sad fact to be an adult,' Denny wondered. Maybe that's why he slept-in the extra five minutes, and why he could feel the sunlight on the shoulder of the poor feck down the road as a sun-chipped razorblade, the card drawn in tarot, its bleeding edge. Kath was probably correct. What he needed was swagger. But as soon as he would acquire himself some swagger, he'd be 'waging a losing bet on the basic tenet of human kind: Colin Farrell got here first. And before that it was John Wayne. And somewhere in between it was Little Richard. (Wait, Little Richard?!).' He had to stop himself from thinking too critically. The nays kept streaming in: 'No Bono, no Premier League stopper, no feckin' Daniel Radcliffe!' It was OK. He'd get up in the morning and if he was a little late for class, if he was a little out of breath, if he knew there was sweat running down the back of his neck, he'd be OK. He'd be OK in his own good time. A trip to Inishdolbe told him so.

Chapter Forty

No rock was out of place, yet it was free to scatter. Something in time had born the earth on which he stood, and he could change it with the kick of his shoe – and it would go on largely unchanged too. The waves rolled over themselves like they were having fun. The air was dank and seal-grey, as if your own vision couldn't penetrate the mirror. Whatever song was being heard wasn't forced. Denny found all the swagger he'd ever need. In the youth hostel, on a borrowed couch because he knew he couldn't pay, he picked up a worn blue book that was between the pillow and the arm called *Why We Feel the Way We Do*. Someone else had been reading, probably secretly. It was signed 'For Maria', whoever she was – she was somewhere, or had been, and hers was an inscribed copy, a paraphrase of a quotation Denny had heard before: 'All people should strive to learn before they die what they are running from and to, and why.' Mr James Thurber. Quote unquote, broke the sky. 'I feel like the sky just opened up,' Denny felt himself conclude. 'But not in rain, in an abundance – maybe just air.'

Denny was in a dream set inside a glass jar. Bits of sand came sputtering in and he felt himself pummelled by kisses that were leaving mild itches on almost every inch of his skin. 'Nulee – ' he tried to voice, but the tongue and the palate produced only a whisper. He felt the air from the atmosphere of his mouth offer a cup to the salt of ocean. He was in a trance, for a second, wishing he'd met Nuala sooner.

In Rathmines, it was always 'Would it be a brand new girl and a Cadillac?' for Denny. Not that he had a thing for Caddies, particularly.

Rounded fenders, sure. Leather seats, sure. Curved trunks and oval hoods, popping grill, hard/soft dash like a leather jacket pressed to a field next to the Cliffs of Moher. Sure. He was a young man, after all. An American boy. He'd admit, in the end, if he had to. How swiftly, though, years later, Denny often retreated to the feeling he had on Lower Rathmines, outside the college, not knowing a soul, and the aroma of American fried chicken wings permeating the sidewalk, where he preferred chips. He wanted Blarney now. Which is to say, he wanted the feeling he had imagining Nuala while he was away from her. Not to say he wanted nothing. He wanted. He wanted something. He wanted some. While the others were rambling about town or stuck in their hotel room playing rummy, or shenanigans, he wanted to be so much older than he was, and also a few years younger, so he could have a chance. Have a chance with the maidens of the prom. Have a chance with the fooling around he never did as much as the others his age or any age. He was a pilgrim who was still a puritan byproduct, lost trying to be a new young man in a far more interesting place. In Dublin they saw straight through it. In Galway he thought he had hope. In Cork he wasn't so sure. In Belfast anything could happen, or it didn't. He had an idea he'd like Limerick! Sligo slid off but he could never let her go.

He remembered a dull afternoon on O'Connell Street when the season's greens, ribbons and sleigh-bells were just being put out on the shutters and columns throughout the more noticeable parts of the city. However, people seemed to be decorating their shops out of obligation, as if a sigh were visible and a heavy hand unavoidable. The fact that there was little enthusiasm in the process could have been due to the light rain, coming on early and shockingly cold. And this was a sign that more, and sleet even, would certainly be expected as colder months wore on. Families had the holidays to look forward to, but there would be a price. There were always costs, and loneliness, and the retailers tried their best to make the conversation about happiness, fulfilment, gaiety (as if the word meant what it was supposed to mean any more). Denny felt damp already; the chill of wind and rain on his cheeks, and the weather slicing through his thin clothes as though he were nothing but a tree. 'But even a tree has more to its trunk than I do,' he thought, belittling himself only because it justified how cold he felt. He'd gone to the GPO to mail a postcard to his parents. It had been a while. He enjoyed being 'nobody's son', just as he imagined the girls he saw after school and in the pubs enjoyed being nobody's daughters. Except they were. Every one of them was. Denny wondered about the orphans. Of course they were somebody's daughters and sons too. No less somebody's. No less their own person. The post office, gleaming as it was on the interior, sagged a little that day. It was not a physical sagging but the weight of the employees – again, not a physical weight but a semblance around the eyes, countenance of shoulders, and a dusting of defused light over their heads, as though they had been here too long. Their mouths dipped at the corners like a cap that wasn't worn, placed over a bannister-knob or on the pile of mail at their homes. It was the heaviness of absence allowing the elbows to sag, and sigh, as only inanimate objects and animals can – as well as plants. 'Everything slopes if given a chance,' Denny's science teacher had taught him. For sure Dublin was sloping for him this night. Night it was, since afternoon couldn't – didn't want to – hang on to the battle. 'Everything slopes.' Sure enough, day and night.

The shopkeepers wished they had gloves as they fussed with wire and trim. Denny was relieved to see the cinema alive, however. Night had allowed this instant infusion of neons – purple and amber, pink and blue – and suddenly there was brightness. The artificial colour made Denny smile a little. Something so simple, such synthetic finery, could move a pedestrian to notice. Without a further thought, Denny was going to the movies. He didn't particularly care about what he'd see, and it seemed to him to be a good idea to be surprised. The hour and a half went by and Denny had forgotten about what he mailed and why. He let be how inconsequential he felt in his clothes, how little muscle he showed even in a tight T-shirt, how inexpensive his shoes were (and it showed, or so he thought; everything was so important to the people who could afford things, especially to people who noticed shoes). The film had been about a teenage girl who, born out of wedlock to a peasant mother, grew up persecuted, until her village was invaded by elements of a ruthless militant drug cartel run by an elite gang of real estate moguls who were also vampire zombies, and she saves herself and her mother, as well as saving the father she never knew (who, it turns out, was the henchman for the cartel – but in the end he is good and proves he never henched anyone but facilitated their freedom instead), and along with them she saves even the bad people who had convicted her in their silence, the village, the whole future civilisation, because through courage against insane odds (and by the fact she is endowed with the grace and ferocity of acrobatic feats, a keen mental agility, and undefiable confidence despite years of being shunned), she becomes an international hero and by her example the rules of dominance are changed, shifting abundance and opportunity to everyone (at which point the film ends – however, a caveat scrolls up on a black screen: 'Abundance to abundance, opportunity to all, temporary love begets the next fall').

Outside the cinema the streetlights and automobiles caused the street to feel like day. The rain had cleared and a thin haze of fog drifted around the lights like the visage of an omen, the presence of which Denny felt entranced to be near. He waited for a bus to pass him and then he crossed the street to the median and stood beside one of the statues. The lights inside old Clerys looked like a palace, and it enticed him. He knew he had some change in his pocket, so he walked up the tall steps like a threadbare galactic senator and proceeded to the café. Although he was wearing blacks and greys, he felt like the good prince-groom; the room was astonishingly white and had absorbed whatever gleam the GPO seemed to have lost in the yellow-aged glower of Denny's chilly quick inspection. He was sure, now, he had misread the post office, and maybe the employees too. He felt so much better after he'd spent time with the teenage-girl hero, stepping into the optimism of commerce at night, and now standing in the polished warm room that invited him – knowing nothing of the amount of money he had in his pockets. This was the good thing about commerce, he observed. You can enter, participate, and leave as anyone – the rich 1 percent or the other 99. As soon as he thought it, he realised its ambiguities, its exceptions, its unequitable flaws. Never mind, for now he was going to be the future prince of Donna – the hero and leader of *Actuwhile*, the vision on the screen.

The hostess at Clerys seated him next to a podium on top of which a large Grecian urn sprouted a delicate fern. About thirty feet away a young woman sat at a raised round table near one of the big windows. A chrome cylinder rose about four feet to meet the table, a seemingly heavy disk that appeared more suitable to cocktails. She sat alone facing Denny's way, and he noticed straight away that she was pretty. She had a cup of tea in a white cup, placed on a white saucer, that matched her book cover. She seemed to be in the middle, although Denny couldn't make out the title. Silver and gold outlined the words. What drew him to her at first were her stockings. She was so high off the ground; the chair-legs were almost as tall as the table, and chrome as well. She sat with her knees touching, like close friends. Denny hadn't seen a woman wearing white stockings since he was a boy – and they weren't women then, they were girls. Back then she would be a choirgirl and he'd be in slacks. 'Slacks.' Not like a Seattle slacker guy, not a surf dude, but a clean-cut young man of good neighbourhood standing. Any father would have picked up the phone and been relieved to hand the call to his daughter if he knew the young man wore *slacks*. The fact was Denny was in jeans, a charity shirt – collared though it was – and a tattered jacket that almost suggested he was of another time. If he were only a visitor on earth he would not be surprised. No one on the planet was as lonesome. The young lady's legs were a softer marble, wrapped in cashmere and angora. Her face intensely studied her book, but Denny could tell she had as much awareness of what was going on around her as on the page. Her mouth welcomed the tea but she had not kissed anyone, he thought, in a rather long time. She seemed to breathe with every sentence, as if she were waiting to be interrupted. It was this easy to fall in love, Denny began to understand again. He was warm with knowing. He hoped she'd be.

Still, there was the past and here was the present. But the future seemed to follow the past and present as if it had to be the bugger to always remind you about what you didn't have. He remembered the pimply ankles, like little covered ears, and the flat greasy bangs from the leisure centre. He'd look down to the dust beneath the tables and then glimpse a straight angle of hairline before looking up to the ceiling. 'Ah, Lard . . . ' he'd pretend back then, 'would you save someone for Denny?'

As Nuala approached where they'd stay for the night, a coin in the ground, or the opposite of O'Connell's stick in the sky: the library dome was moon-snailish, a milky nipple uncovered in the earth, some aspect of a giant adored queen the legends of Swift could have conjured to rally all of Ireland, once uncovered. But it was the earth's, merely and mostly and mightily – architectural eye be known. The rise reminded them of Marco Polo's portable palace, although it was said Marco's was bamboo, a royal backpacker's weather-resistant pop-up sanctuary, a Chinese dragon setting down in the middle of a street during a parade. While the emperor was on safari in the sheltered wild park of his own walled kingdom, his lacquered shell harnessed with thick silk ropes would hold down the top to festivities (a harem, Denny saw in the print of Nuala's blouse; a small place where the dancers started to induce trances particular and peculiar to the imagination). When the rain went slack, the water hit their shoulders and cheeks like a rain-jacket suddenly flung in the wind.

Intermittently they saw the light blue and cloud white of a gorgeous day, but where they were gave them a workout. The land was drenched, and soon they were too. The dome shed the rain like a sheer fountain. Rainfall slithered down the glass and immersed itself in every direction inside the grass around the underground hotel. A patch of view showed the ocean heavy in white brows, and they were thankful to get themselves inside. They caught their breath and the hot air of their little struggle combined with what the stove gave in a central pit below the dome and showed them to be sweaty. The layers of Gore-Tex, rubber, cotton, wool, and wicking material were beginning to beg to be released. There were showers upstairs, down a cedar-lined hallway in a small room with tiny white tiles that were only slightly larger than teeth — well-brushed teeth. They were nowhere but here. Not in a Cadillac, not in a bungalow on a beach in South Africa, not back in the States painting a fence, and not in Dublin being reminded of darker times.

Chapter Forty One

For the first time in months they'd heard from Sarge. Ebola was breaking out all over the African continent, so the news reported, but Sarge said he hadn't seen a single case. 'Big continent,' Denny remarked. 'He better be lucky,' Nuala insisted. They'd slept the night under the vast wooden skirt of hobbitdom and woke to the smell of oatmeal and fresh bread. As Denny was back on coffee, he had to wait, but Nuala enjoyed her tea while they traded glances in the intimate throng of other guests, most of whom they hadn't seen until they'd reached the basement cafeteria. All the travellers were reading maps and laughing in small groups of two to four, talking about what lay ahead. Nuala and Denny would return, by the carriageway, to Dublin – but only after one brief adventure southerly, upon an island.

'Sarge probably told us that so we'd be calm.'

'Yep, and it seemed to work!'

They drove on, Nuala again at the wheel, and Denny's eye went to where Denny's eyes would go. To road and turns, to cautions, and to the edges of Nuala's lips, eyes, cheekbones, clothes. They listened to a radio station that seemed to imitate a radio station from thirty years ago. They laughed at the lyrics – 'Ridiculous!' – and the simple melodies and bass beats. 'Nick who?' Of course it mattered to Nick but the music belonged to a generation that, in ways they could imagine – because they knew what in the world had changed and they knew what hadn't – made a mark on their time, present time, passing along the road, as was true. Even the towns they drove through looked thirty years old. 'Thirty, forty, five hundred!' Nuala said – and by no means an exaggeration. Keyes Butcher stayed open past six. There must be a big event somewhere in town. Crimpson's crimson and gold storefront wanted to be grand but after hours it stood forlorn. Its stiff awning seemed a fright, a modern mask of what store or pub – or family home – used to be at this address. McMooney's funeral parlour looked like a grotto, in a former house of ill-repute. At the corner by the bus-lane, a soldier home from duty waited next to grandmothers and retired men. Denny could see Sarge in the young man's uniform. Darkness was flat across the sky.

'Denny, my man, you'd fit in well at Black Mary's . . . ' Sarge had told him outside the leisure centre after Denny had been feeling bad about himself.

'Black as rain,' Denny shot back.

Of course he meant the Chapel of Ease, a silly name for such a desperate condition.

Kath was right: he had to loosen up. Ease on down whichever road he was going to be on.

He started to drift, and Nuala nudged him awake. They had singing to do. 'Nik Kershaw, is it?' They helped the radio finish the song.

When a funeral place looks too enchanting, that's probably the time to talk to the Father, Holy Mother, and Joseph. But what about for the Buddhist? What if you're Muslim? What if you don't believe in anything? Who do you talk to then? The Sister, the Brother, the rolling hills?

There was that brook in Sligo and the Ha' Penny Bridge wasn't too far. There was water, plenty. Generations, too many maybe, had found it in the pubs.

He thought Sarge was making it all right. He knew Kath was doing fine. Mick was probably doing double duty on side-by-side mattresses.

Denny looked at Nuala, her thigh showing a little. They had passed the funeral shop, they were beyond need of the butcher, and they were motoring home – like the runner on second, as they'd say about baseball players in America, readying to steal for third, touch the bag and round the bend for home.

Chapter Forty Two

He didn't have to stay in the flat along the Dodder forever. He knew this. Time away had been good. Sitting on the banks, the grass not yet sharp or dry, the sunshine felt like the remediation of something good. He began to review his impressions and closed his eyes. A cooler breeze worked under the sun and rode the current on top of the Dodder. What he thought was a funeral home was a post office. The sexy lady in the town by the fair was petting her shepherd. In a store near the surfers: denim jeans, muck boots, camel-hair scarf, spring jacket. Through woods they passed: a white script, breast of deer, loading dock for meat in the next town, and a freezer, unseen. They rattled up next to each other, a scrum to sniff truffles, sea-lion rock smooth and swirls off the coast looking at the dots of islands. Slip beneath ice at the floe under falls. A maid's dress in the entrance to a hotel, her head in the stairs. Bone of building, canal, beam through the centre tunnels cracked. Granite wedges through the never-mind of commerce, river out racing yesteryear's trains. The jittery seat. Carriage on the anklet of the barista at Strandhill. Under the library dome, no pyre yet but that grain. Glacier's still swathe through intimate sun-spots; through the rocks. The man outside the bar: 'We'll never forget what's-his-name.' Another joke in Galway: 'A man gets up at the bar.' Zigzag eddies teasing land under trees through solid trunks until it hits the marble no one sees. Parnell. Oyster, filth, ragged cloth, shiner, the citizenship of actors walking away from the pub.

Someone had planted orchids, and near them a Japanese maple. Denny observed that the maple lifted its skirts to the fountain. Just then

Nuala called. He had been almost asleep when the fountain entered his vision and Nuala called not five seconds after. She'd come down to where he was, and from there they'd figure out where to go next. They began to miss their holiday as soon as they landed back in Dublin, but they felt refreshed, relaxed, and they conjured everything good about the weekend in a few minutes – hoping to make it last.

*

The *Indie Book Review* arrived in Monday's mail and Nuala brought it inside to their small round kitchen table near one of the back windows. She put down the telephone bill, the quarterly newsletter from the Lord Mayor, the Donegal Pride season's fashions catalogue, and handed Denny a modest book with a red wheelbarrow on the cover inside a plastic wrapper. Den' opened the perforated top and slid the publication out. On page five was this fragment, from 'Cities Unvisited' by a Mr Richard Gwyn: 'He experienced an epiphany: It was not Alexandria he was looking for, but another city, a place that he would have to invent.'

Denny's 'Egypt' was never far from the top of his bucket-list, and over one particularly long and romantic night Denny and Nuala discussed 'the Alexandrias of our imaginations' well into morning. For the entire week after they researched the Egyptian cat, the mau, on a hunch Miss Mau would help fulfil their mutual affections for travel and history, vicariously, and add a new member to their little family along the Dodder. Whether they stayed at Strand Terrace or not didn't matter, though they thought they'd always stay. At least this was the *always* of early adulthood. Things could change, and they knew this – not with each other, although there's always that depressing possibility in today's world. Depressing or exciting, some people thought – such as the radio announcers and the millionaire geniuses of online dating.

Sometimes they wished they'd lived off Earl Street – back in the day of the tramway. Denny could suit up for work and hang off the edge like a skateboarder dude pursuing a life of dreams and leisure, while pulling down a good and honest living from a city-centre firm. (This would be Nuala's tease, not an actual dream of Denny's.) Nuala could catch the early tram to the Liberties and have herself a bench-seat for a sure fifteen minutes of reading. The domestic things couldn't come fast enough once they'd reached eighteen, and at twenty-one they were physically yearning to identify the things they loved. Once arranged, these preferences would symbolise the sophistication and depth of their cosmopolitan acquisitions ('Just like Hemingway in Havana,' Denny affirmed when he found a strange thing he was keen on at one of the more exotic charity shops, 'I'll let my friends hang their hats on the sharp tip of an antelope!' Of course Sarge changed this a bit, and instead of antelope 'tip' he liked to say Denny's guests would hang it on the same, starting with a 't,' only it rhymed with 'bit'). Sarge had always imagined he'd 'retire' to Booterstown, and never have to live near the barracks again. 'Every day the Irish Sea, Den',' Sarge dreamed aloud between shots, as he cleaned up the table down to the eightball. 'And it's not long from Ballsbridge to Donnybrook, Den'; I mean, it's not far from Donnybrook Court to Beaver Row . . . ' Though Denny knew what he meant, he thought – something about suddenly having a house with six kids – he also thought it was rare that Sarge used a euphemism.

'Good for Sarge,' Denny declared to himself.

From Finglas to the Rathmines barracks to Temple Bar, he was moving up. Wasn't he? Well, if to say these things is 'moving up'. 'Good for Sarge.' 'Sexist Sarge, more like,' Nuala would say, if she could hear Denny's thoughts. Although she was half-kidding.

It was hard not to like Sarge. 'The soldier who wouldn't hurt a flea.' He was almost a cartoon of himself. Nuala and Denny missed him, especially every time they passed Donnybrook Court or Blackrock.

It would be a long while – many months, even years – before Sarge returned from the UN coalition tour. He was making good money and 'doing good' to boot. Maybe he would make it to Booterstown after all. But Nuala and Denny kept their dreams a little open, like a stage-set with many scrims in the fly-space for scenes – much as they enjoyed making home along the Dodder.

Sarge had been there for Denny when a young guy at the leisure centre gave Denny a rough time over something he'd overheard. Denny had told Sarge about the time Denny was in a talent show, as a kid, and the boy at the next pool table leaned over and whispered into Denny's ear, 'Miss *Lovely*, Miss *Lovely*' – only it sounded to Denny like '*Low*-very, *Low*-very.'

'You ain't so lovely yourself, now get on and find your own craic,' Sarge told the guy. And that was the end of that.

*

It was back near Earl Street – between the man with the cane and summer vacation, you could say – that Denny happened to see Bono, from the famous band, and a young girl called out to the Edge and said, the way only a smartass kid with courage could yell: 'How famous *are* you, mister?' Inside his thoughts, Denny commented, 'Like the degrees of fame mattered!' Denny identified with the kid and he identified with the musician, strangely enough. He'd wanted to be somebody too. And the kid, it seemed, already *was* 'somebody'. Bold, to be bold. Good for the kid. But whether it was Van or Bono or holy cow Mother Teresa, most people wouldn't remember. This was the sad thing. One group replacing the other. Denny saw the beginnings of it now. Would the old man in the shop without lights at the top of the stairs – the virtually homeless tailor – be replaced by now? The pizza shop – Dreamin' of New York – would it be gone to expensive condos; would the new residents eat caviar instead? Would the rhino be replaced by an elephant? They were all worthy creatures and poachers wanted their blood: rhino, turtle, elephant. It could have been any of them in the Dodder but, no, it wasn't the elephant and it wasn't the turtle – whose blood, went the claim, cured anaemics, the infertile, and the worst-off.

What Denny would become, if he could determine this, was still an open question – like 'an open boat without any manifest at the moment', as Sarge described himself when Denny'd asked him if he was scared, being enlisted in the Irish army, of facing a tour of duty. Yet, they were all young and, except for the Saint, there was no reason to believe a car on Drury Street, for example, would lash out and buck them in the gullet and sanctify their fate in the gutter. Kath would go on to be cyrogenicised or robotically cloned if she could. She has the vision and the gumption, Sarge observed. 'Nualee would be Nualee wherever she went.' Heavens would open their doors, and curtains and picnic blankets would float down like a hundred thousand cats in slo-mo, all purring an' meowing, finally – like they were about to spend a pleasant afternoon on Mary Pickford's shoulder, morphing into one good kitty. Mick would catapult himself into space where in the galaxies beyond he'd find he could live eternally as a hundred-year-old cowboy.

Denny watched the sunlight though the bead plant in the northwest corner of the potter's cottage that was easily ignored. He had named the plant 'Jimmy J' partly because the plant seemed as forlorn as any of the statues of Joyce he'd seen, and partly because the beads reminded him of dreadlocks. 'J' just seemed appropriate for hanging there, the little end a nubby hook, no sharp attack. Shiva's Tandava would probably have been a better name – although Denny wasn't sure the bead plant could resolve the universe's comings and goings any more than he could. Yet, maybe this is what the Saint had – unbeknown to himself – tried to do through dance. And maybe this is why his dance ended up . . . elsewhere. All those classes and lolly-gagging! Not by a huge stretch of the imagination did the bead plant dance a little. The shifting light, the same light lessened only by a curled crown of trees, was wavering into the sands of Sandymount in the very same moment. He knew he had to water it only once every two weeks and he felt sorry to admit he didn't always remember. Poor plant. In another place, a different time, an exotic country where beads and dreads are customary, his potter's-cottage bead plant would be cared for better, maybe even revered. Why not? Plenty of people name their plants, just as they name their dogs and cats and deformities. Kath's ivy 'Robert' was thriving as a surrogate lover. (So she admitted to Sarge under duress of extreme punchiness one night at the Village on Wexford Street. Sarge and Kath had been clubbing without their fair share (the others!) one lonesome night before Sarge shipped off to Nigeria with his unit. Elated and drained at the same time, she admitted things to Sarge she hadn't ever told Denny. For Sarge, this was a big dial-up on the social register between friends. She didn't tell him what she did with the leaves, but he did ask, you can be sure of it. 'And it wasn't all poison?' Sarge thought he's landed the boyfriendly-brotherly jab-tease that might make her smile so wide she'd have to include him – maybe even as much as a boyfriend. Possible? This was one of Sarge's most appealing characteristics: nothing much daunted him – and quite a lot of social rejection eluded him.)

Chapter Forty Three

It was said that at the back of the Village you could sometimes have a new bride if you danced hard enough. Although the street had been there a lot longer than the bar, New Bride Street took on the allure of risky business barely two blocks away. As it happened, this is where Kath was living before Denny and Sarge met her. Kath on New Bride Street with a tiger cat and a teapot, both of which she cherished: they had been given to her by her grandmother. The 'Celtic Tiger'? That, Kath liked to joke, started in her kitchen ('Between a kitty and wail,' Denny added, to be smug and provocative, having heard his share of New Bride Street stories.) 'Blame me, lads. I'm the lass!' Kath said, mockingly, placing extra emphasis on the last three characters of 'lass'.

'At last a little honesty,' Sarge said, poking fun of financiers and government, he thought.

They all wished they'd had more dance, more clubbing, more Village nights extended to New Bride Street and well beyond.

'Well, what did Lorde do down in New Zealand for fun with her friends?' Denny put to his friends, as if to incite a proposal among them for some novel idea.

'Municipal transportation with only a pocket-full of change,' Sarge said dryly.

'They *made* fun with quite a bit of little,' Nulee offered. She was, after all, the most *catholic* among them. Once, for her fourteenth birthday, her grandmother ordered a blouse from Grants – usually it was all they could do to save for Lynch's – and she wore the socks for years, mum stitching the toes to last a couple of months longer.

'You fuks, it's the story of every adolescence!' Kath said, speaking of making little with nothing and riding around on public transport.

'I bet there's a bit better going on down in Beggar's Bush,' Sarge said ruefully – or so it seemed to Kath. He would have been stationed there in another century . . . grand arch and all . . . but he probably wouldn't have met Kath and Denny, the Saint and Nulee.

Today, though, Nuala and Denny would go to Press, the café at Garrison Chapel, and while splurging on avacado, corn, potato and prawn soup, Denny would think of Listons, and the 'old' days. The greenhouse at the National Print Museum reminded him of his potter's cottage.

It's as if the self in the self is always with the self, Denny was thinking. 'You can never get out of yourself, even if you change,' he muttered into his soup.

'It's the fun of one package . . . ' Nuala said, suggesting a range of skills and accumulated knowledge, oncoming fashions and vintage attributes.

'I like our potter's cottage, Den'.' She knew what Denny was getting at, and went straight for his feeling. She'd seen his eyes swirl upwards and around to indicate that even though they were on a walk, an outing even, settling for a 'fancy' lunch with the museum crowd, that they'd in a sense come back to the same place, the same *looking* place as where they drew their day and night: framed by glass and skeletal architecture, the potter's cottage and the Dodder was now even more of a clock.

'Will we grow old together, you think?' Denny wanted to know, and asked hopefully.

He liked the chunks of prawn and the amount of butter in the cream. The chef had sprinkled an ample amount of parsley, as if to cover a patch of playing field that had been scuffed up by virtue of a goal, and Denny smiled, remembering what Sarge would say, pressing his lips together while staring at Nuala. 'Whhhaaaat?' She stirred.

'You don't eat parsley,' he said firmly.

'Of course you do, mister!' came her swift reply. It was as much Denny's, and the Saint's, as it was Sarge's. Besides, he liked parsley.

'You'd nev'r be far from the maternity hospital,' Sarge would enjoy pointing out.

'Doesn't have to be!' sprung Kath.

You couldn't argue with either.

They got kind of excited imagining the Heidelberg printer, stamping hand-fed onion skin. 'A crowning achievement!' mocked Denny.

'A gripper delivery, carried out and released!' Nuala teased, imitating the docent's wee excited whisper.

'Ah, yes, and yes: *realised*,' Denny underscored thematically.

'Once is never enough,' compiled Nuala on top of the argument.

'Let us hope,' Denny commanded, taking Nuala's inner palm into the press of his fingers, pulling her closer to him.

Maybe someday they would have their own crowning achievements, times some, but for now they were enjoying the privilege of fooling around somewhere between teens and adulthood – still, even with their own address together. They had time in the future for crowning achievements and there was plenty to be gripped elsewhere, in the present.

Every bush gave a nod, it seemed, as Denny and Nuala passed the hedges toward Lansdowne Road. Their little stems flung themselves forward and back quite like the Heidelberg machine. The walking brought them closer. Denny thought he'd have to take a pee pretty soon, a captain jack around the next corner. The mason jar of whatever he'd had under the warmth of Press, sweetened celery juice or something with 'Mumbo' in the title, now felt like a jar of sand, and he wished the grains would be released, one at a time – but quickly. The bushes didn't affect Nuala in quite the same way, but she felt free to be outside – and the sound of the Heidelberg oiled and geared did slip memory into some anticipated action. They felt like fifteen-year-olds again: heart-rate almost double what it should be at rest, but now all the time – through every class. It was hard to concentrate. If a classmate kissed one of them they'd be all there, all over it, in an instant. They'd allow themselves to be sloppy. Uniforms creased. A locker is a fine cool wall for heat; slippery board, like a surfer's, and slippery floor that the custodian had waxed the night before. Better to think about the rhino, Denny figured. No, no, no, not the rhino.

He felt the bulge of his phone and Nuala commented at the next turn that she was getting cold up top and wished she'd worn a sweater. 'A red sweater signals weather,' Denny said – half his breath missing. The urge to get to the sand was fighting the ferocity of the wind to make them stay. Every step made them feel like magnets. They knew they adored each other in nine out of ten of the right ways.

The toilet seat of the Aviva Stadium was glimmering like an armadillo. The way it squatted was sexy, Denny felt, and besides it shimmered more like abalone under the spots of clouds mottling the earth as breeze sprinted in from Wicklow. Denny hadn't known the shape for long, only the shine looked familiar – like a coin. However, the shape didn't take long to recognise, just as he figured the Saint would have told him, although it would take a lifetime to get to know. He wanted to be that bird, a plover from scallop rig to the stadium's incline, sitting there with all of time, patient for the catch. Only he wasn't feeling so patient. He *was*, just as he was when he was fifteen, sixteen, lord-god seventeen and eighteen! Now it was as if he was carrying a bowling-ball case of sand and he could pee a tunnel. He dared not mention all of it to Nuala because he knew from experience some of it would surely turn her off. 'It's just *language*,' Denny would propose. Nah. It wouldn't do if she wasn't ready. He respected that but he also knew Nuala would love to reconcile their affinities for avocado and prawn, celery and pasta. He felt sure he could get beyond parsley.

They went back, taking a right on Herbert to Serpentine. The breeze won. The fly between windows won. Their relief was to get back home. The flat was cool and so were their cheeks and legs. Hungry, for some reason so soon after lunch at Press – although they had walked at a quickened pace – in the cold room Nuala reached for the apple and it, too, on Denny's nightside table was cold to touch. In her mouth the white flesh dripped cool and quenched her thirst. She offered the bite to Denny and it seemed already a pool, at least a crater, that was warming but moist. The apple tasted good. He'd had them, plucked from trees, in Ohio and New Hampshire and Maine. This apple was so much more smooth on the outside. It slipped in his hand and landed on his thigh. 'Red as St Mary's,' Nuala said.

A bowl of lemons waited for them on the kitchen table and the good vitamins in them, although bitter, made them think they could run a marathon. They talked about going back to Sligo or about seeing another part of the country. The Giant's Causeway, even. 'You'll have the Ring of Kerry anytime,' Nuala said with sleepy eyes. 'Your favourite caps are made there,' she reminded him.

'Or Sligo back down to Cobh,' Denny added with twinkling eyes. 'Then Kinsale.'

It was as if the cork had been let out of the bottle. They both knew. They were having fun, the way they should have had when they were teenagers. The sounds of words so good on their tongues. It was as if they commanded a language now. And nobody but themselves was grading them on their sentences.

The neighbour's musical choices, likely Pandora-driven, pulsated through the north wall. They would be well off at only twenty-two, and they'd own the whole neighbourhood pretty soon. To dream so far ahead, suddenly Nuala and Denny's days along the Dodder seemed numbered, but it simply didn't matter. They had the day. And they had the next. And this was all, when you're in love, that really mattered.

It wasn't like America here. Even with all the Irish in America – and Americans claiming Ireland – the worlds seemed far away, Denny observed. Outside, he flicked an acorn into the river. The little cap bobbled, almost sank, and became a compass on the current. It remained in sight, spiralling, for several minutes, and then a swift Wicklow gust sent it toward the big pool. He noticed there was no map to 'split' the river unequally, the way some rivers were divided on American maps. The Connecticut river, for example, would belong more to Holden Caulfield's granite state than to the green mountains that seemed to give it at least half its glory in measure. Maybe the Mississippi was like this too. 'Land sakes!' Denny's relatives back home would say. You'd think a river could be a river in no one particular state. Rivers flow where they want and will. Denny was thinking, *Very 'Walden, very Huck Finn and Tom Sawyer – very* Paddle-to-the-Sea. No politics warred over which side of the Dodder was claimed. Of course, except for its origins, it was *all Dublin* – and there could be no disputing the bounds over which, or under which, the Dodder would flow. To one side, ocean told the river it was near. To the other side, one periphery of the interior of Irish civilisation loomed as it gathered before the great cross of midland towns and fields until the great waist of the nation funnelled into the Atlantic at the cliffs and craggy rocks, the trickling stream heads in moist banks, the dirt or stones that made teethmarks in the land or else their numbers. *No one owns the Dodder! The Dodder decides the Dodder!* Denny was comfortable with this robust lack of restraint, even if the river allowed itself to be seemingly penned in here and there. The waters would never need to be 'liberated' by Kingstown. No kings or queens had any bearing here, just as they didn't with the *Mayflower*. And no, Neville Francis Fitzgerald Chamberlain didn't invent snooker any more than Indians did. (He may have *played* the game, sure.) The rivers invented it! And now politics reflect it.

Nuala joined him, poking her arm through the loop of his own, held like a teacup due to his habit of walking with a hand in his jeans pocket, when he wasn't eating nuts or using his phone.

'Every walker on earth has a story,' says Nuala.

'Or anywhere,' says Den.

'What do you mean?' says she.

'*Any* walker *anywhere*,' repeats he.

'Ohhh. I see. Yes. Yes, indeed. You're speaking to potential, aren't y', Den'?

They made habits of small moments, tiny differences that did not matter. It was a game with language, but it was as much, and more, a game involving their tongues. *Twister. Sister.* They went on like this along their walks. *Bark. Dog. Up . . . The wrong tree!*

It felt like ages since he was the boy freezing in the flat along the East Wall, where there was nothing but the Irish Sea's fierce wind across the private cricket club field. A few clothes hung over a useless bedframe the Saint had set against the wall under the window provided a little 'insulation'. This was laughable. Sarge had imagined the Yanks lived like Beverly Hills' princes and princesses, but even he was a little shocked by their squalor. The rotisserie just inside the main door, in what would constitute a living room, heated the whole place – only, a warm orb at the level of knees, it didn't make it past the front door or the end of the couch. The boys' room was the furthest back, and in the middle of the hallway was a small kitchen that held a small electric stove and oven that couldn't heat a Cornish hen. Soups it would heat. So many weeks of soups, from cans, and it was easy to understand why Denny looked forward to gyros with the special sauce every other Thursday on allowance day.

He would feel a damp circulating air around his body and wonder how ice had formed between his sweatshirt and the interior of his old sleeping bag as he slept. One eye opened first. The Saint was already up and in the kitchen – quite unlike how he'd be slumped over in a classroom chair. Something, Denny wondered, was getting the Saint out of bed each morning in a flash, and Denny figured it must be a girl. 'Who else has to go to school earlier than we do?' Denny calculated. He'd seen the Saint do double-takes at the swarm of girls coming off the bus and walking in pairs and threes and fours down Portobello and Rathmines. The young women's sodality was a mob in saunter and affect but the Saint seemed entranced. And yet he never let himself get so far gone in fantasy – the groom putting key to the flat before the shoes, always able to narrow his gaze to the one or two who had potential: they could go for him. He got lots of looks this way, and sometimes the gaggle turned into a group giggle. One among them would turn a handsome chin over her shoulder, flouncing her sweater trim and hapless reel of skirt before swishing the arrow of her body back into the rest of the pod. It was this sort of interaction that must have gotten the Saint up early on school days and given him the confidence that something satisfying would result from his hanging out at the leisure centre.

They liked to walk. It felt like an Irish tradition even though most of the born-and-raised Irish Denny knew preferred to sit. 'Our ancestors walked from the invaders no faster than they walked the land for grain, for rock, for spuds and peat,' Nuala said with pride. She didn't mean the ancestors were cowards. Quite the opposite. 'We're an unafraid people, Denny' – a point that was true in every example – 'Except,' as Denny quickly pointed out, 'when dating a Yank.'

'Ah, there you have it! But you found someone, no?'

'And did it take a soldier, a saint and a lesbian to do it?'

'I suppose. No matter the fashion, you found me.'

Chapter Forty Four

The notion of *found* was what Denny had been looking for. He thought he'd 'found' home away from home in Dublin but hindsight was making him wonder whether or not his particular Rathmines had roughed him up. And which 'Bloom' was he, anyway? Jayzus, he felt too lascivious for a kid still clinging to his teens. But he felt older than his skin and hair and clothes at times too. Which Bloom was the Saint, or Sarge, or any of them for that matter? 'There's an old man in every . . .' No. This didn't sound right. Surely Kath could be a Bloom, and Nuala too. What's the female equivalent to a man who wanders and wants?

'Joan of Arc,' Nulee said.

'I suppose,' Denny agreed. He added, 'Sinead . . . ?' and Nuala gave him a look.

'You love the quivery voice, don't you, Den'.'

'Supposin' I do?' Denny challenged on the amorous side, a side that was still new to him. 'Would you quiver then?' he said with his best local emphasis.

'Um, maybe. Maybe I'd *quaver*, Den',' Nuala replied. She meant to rhyme his name with 'then', but also to give the nod to Denny *himself*. And if they were anywhere else, she might have replaced it all with '*now*'. He wasn't sure why a girl who'd been schooled so repressively could grow up to be so unrepressed, at least at certain moments. He didn't know girls like that back home. At least he never got as far as knowing them beyond the surfaces. It wasn't the world that was naïve, it was himself. It wasn't Nuala who was so old-school. She was the opposite. And Sarge wasn't a bloodthirsty warrior at all, but a kind-hearted beast. Denny was naive to believe that one person's blooming, as he'd have it, was as simple as wandering and wanting. Ask women. And yet it's all true.

'You seem to be on a mini-mini-walkabout here today, Den',' Nuala observed.

'Aye, I am,' Denny teased, in a Popeye sort of way. 'Always. Anywhere and always.'

'And it's a reason I love you, love.'

He was glad to hear it but he, presently, was wondering where the Saint had gone to wander.

'I'd say not heaven exactly, but maybe a planet,' Nuala suggested. It was something that Denny had thought before but hadn't explored in public.

'You know those images of the solar system?'

'A swirl, a doughnut of particles?'

'Maybe somewhere out there.'

'Maybe somewhere out there. I can see it happening.'

'And if *you* can see it, *he* can see it, no?'

'Oh dear . . . ' said Denny. The tangled sheets, the maths mistakes, the wrong road while getting lost, dancing around the rim instead of just going for it, the wasted day, sleeping in – snooze upon snooze, forgetting to vote, the unset goal, the unnamed maid, the trip that was blundered, the times that anger blew, the foregone sips never renewed, the battened hatch, the inane retributions, years of social revenge, millions of people dying in a snub, big deaths and little deaths, a turned face, poor decisions and over-thinking, a pot boiling down the final alarm . . .

'My . . . ' doubled Nulee. They'd rather not think about the details. Probably the Saint had already seen too much.

'Much of it good – think of that, Denny.' The veggie momos around the world, but especially from their favorite Tibetan place. Snow on stiff green branches. The healthy fox crossing fields, outwitting the hounds. A living thing in low warm light with shadows, such as a birch tree – or nude. Guitar played like Hendrix from a home-made rig involving an oil-can on Grafton Street. The films you got to see, your face lit like at the fireside; the iceberg and Goldberg combined, 'making a splash', causing your chest to feel full of oxygen – like you're in love with something passing before you now. The tangle in the sheets. Soap. The honeyed smell of soap. How soft a moon-snail is. Light as a bird's wing. How much of it we don't see. Wouldn't it be pleasure to drop in on that?

*

The next day Denny went out to Sandymount and walked the strand as far as he could. He wondered about the people caught by surprise out by the lake. The story of Narcissus came to mind like a flash of his own face in the trick of shallow waters. He thought, better an empty lorry than an individual. He thought, what if when I'm a father – if I'm a father – I'm so busy making our castle in sand, the tide swells up around my little family? But it would never happen. Not the 'father' part but the 'farther'. Maybe the Saint would. Maybe Kath could. Maybe Sarge would manoeuvre out of it as if it were just another military training – and 'fun'. Nuala loved it out there, around the saltwater lake especially. 'The eye of the world,' she'd say, and Denny would let her get away with it, even though he wanted to correct her: 'You mean the eye of the *bay* . . . .' But it was a kind of eye of the world, and sometimes as the tide came in the eye appeared to be crying. Upsetting, it was, to imagine a family caught out there. Or a single old lady. The chances of it seemed impossible though he'd heard it had happened. A lorry, then. A lorry could be lost. Carry it out to the pits of the sea or bury it in place, packing it with sand. The fish'll come. Then the divers, the oysters, and someone would be eating it on their table.

He trudged along the sand past Martello Tower and felt sad for the grin of the bay window that looked like it was wearing braces. He could live there, he told himself for a second. He'd have to cover up when walking from the bathroom to the window, however, he said to himself. 'But why?' came his more daring self. 'You'd be a rock star, and nothing touches you in the moonlight.' Sure. Sure, all right. He'd be 'a rock star' – and nothing would touch him in the moonlight, or any other time. This would never happen. It could have happened to the Saint. Actually, it was happening to the Saint – on a small level. Anthony could glide into a café and heads would turn. He'd go to the head of the queue and someone would have offered him an audition or an all-expenses-paid trip to a place like Bellagio or Dubai. He'd heard Bellagio was at the cunt of Lake Como, and ferries came there. This sounded like an awful joke Sarge would say, right out of the barracks. 'You'll have *mine rath*, Mr *Kurt*, if you bust another "joke", you call it, like that!' Denny heard Kath jab at Sarge. No one ever called him by his actual name but Kath occasionally called him out, using his baptised name as her secret weapon. Next would be Communion – although they'd never asked for this name, funnily enough.

The fact was, Lake Como was a person. You could see it clearly on any map and from any satellite. Sarge wouldn't be pointing out anything anyone else hadn't already noticed and even said out loud. We need friends to say things aloud that we'd think but never say. Like Lady's Cove. Cockel Lake. Poolbeg. He wanted to be down around San Giovanni, just enough to tickle the soft thigh and then see what happens. 'It's too easy, Den,' the Saint would tell him, 'to slide the slippery slope of "distractions".' Yet he, the Saint, was one of the most distracted of all! *How's this fair?* Denny thought to himself. *One person's 'distractions' will be another's 'permissions.'*

He walked so he couldn't see the baths any more, for this was a distraction even when his back was to them. He was still barely old enough to call himself emancipated, and a picture on the side of a bus could cause his imagination to stir. 'Is this what boys are?' Kath asked incredulously one time along the canal. ''Fraid so, Kath. This is what boys are. At least, I suppose, most of us.' Kath was happy with his admission. The truth between them was sacred. She'd never known a boy like Denny.

The clouds darkened into a pearl that had been mixed with soot. It was also the sort of grey that could lead to distraction. Why had he been given this 'gift' of distraction, so much? 'You imagine *anything*,' Kath told him at the teeny table that was at the behest of the lavender man. 'One night in Rathgar and I can't take you *anywhere*!' she declared, sipping her soda. Sarge said, 'You should try living in barracks . . . ' and then he crossed his heart like he was saving himself but didn't really want to.

Chapter Forty Five

Too much joy moves in unexpectedly and it revives the soul. But why should this be too much? Wouldn't this be just right? Why is a word that begins with 'c' and ends in 't' and unites in the middle with a mini version of the UN be considered obscene? 'Girls and women don't like it,' Kath declared firmly. 'Oh, I see . . . ' Sarge picked up, 'if "girls and women" don't like a street sign then they're going to tear it down?'

'I didn't say we'd tear anyt'ing down, Sarge' – this time letting her family notes provide against any doubt where she was born and raised, through and through. True. One word's like a canal, another's as bad as a bad man in a bank, others are banned on gravestones and on the radio.

'What's with this world?' thought Denny, well beyond the tower.

He could see the tiny red blinking lights of the generators: 'Nipples on steeples, candy canes with holding pains,' Sarge would say. Only . . . everyone else had thought it too. Just like the tour guides tell the tourists on O'Connell Street. Just as friends tell friends. There were seasons when Kath wanted to tear it down too but she was, as she would say, 'Too humanist about it.' It was her standard way of ending any discussion that could have ended poorly. He wished he could stop thinking about Lake Como but soon the image turned to Matisse. This is how he could justify it as a minor distraction: Matisse had been there, he was sure, for the lady – if she was a lady – was the cutting image. (He thought this was a skilful use of language amid a walk on sand, amid distraction, amid seeing in his mind's eye Henri Matisse cutting out his lithe blue lady dancers . . . and Denny quickly substituted the word 'spitting' – which

172

admittedly would have worked in the Bellagio context – to 'cutting' ...
which, unfortunately or fortunately for him, also worked.) He was
pleased with this and his habit or gift, whatever you wanted to call it, was
usually a charm that was never told. Nuala had wind of it. Kath knew it
out of hand. And Sarge and the Saint and Mick clearly contributed. 'It's
the sound, Den',' Sarge said. 'It's the sound grunts make.'

Whatever. It didn't matter. It didn't matter and it did. Denny had
never read a banned book that he was aware of. He didn't need to. Sarge
and others provided enough 'banned' material – and Kath's mouth, for
all her goody-goody on people who offended her, gave plenty of samples
herself. This was the joy of Dublin and this was the joy of all of Ireland,
for this matter. You could be downstairs in the pubs or upstairs in the
choir-lofts and still 'they'd *sing*!' noted Nuala's mum when Denny'd been
invited for the third time to have supper at Nuala's house. For a prim
lady to admit to this sort of singing was, well, to the topic: eye-opening.
Of course Denny had encountered the opposites too. The time he called
that girl's number from the leisure centre; there was no going anywhere,
anytime, from father or mother. Probably from sister or brother too.
This was the drag of it. Why couldn't she have had her own phone? Tight
family! On the one side anything goes and everything went. On the
other it was stagnation or iron doors gridlocked in widows' black lace.
He recognised the irony of it: a 'stag' 'nation'. And which widows' black
lace, anyway? Oh, it was getting terrible. Naughty or not, it was knotty
terrain, and Denny blamed his newly adopted country – which was not
new, really, and would know better.

'Americans have worse mouths,' Kath proffered once.

'Oh yeah?' replied Denny. He couldn't deny there were some foul-
lipped politicians and pop stars in the States, but still he heard what he
heard coming from the gentle and sartorial tongues of ordinary Irish in
practically all the places he had visited. It wasn't that the language was
constant, but it was constantly on their minds. 'Forgive me father for I
have . . . '; he thought this but did not say it beyond his larynx. First of
all, Denny had a hard time conceiving of 'Father' with the capital 'F'
without only thinking about his own dad. No other father was his. The
father half the people seemed to refer to as God – if you asked about
what he fathered and then you got into the Book of Genesis ('A book
of genius, if you ask me!' said Sarge around the pool table when the
conversation turned toward 'Great Beginnings') – well, this Father of All

was farther than Denny could imagine, especially after the Saint was let go. 'To say nothing of the larynx,' Kath illustrated for them all once they were feeling comfortable and settled in that night at Tibet House. She had a fondness for the larynx, as did Nuala. Anything to keep the subject low and the spirits high, Denny realised.

It was terrible to be a post-teen, on your own, in a city where the streets are named 'Dame' and 'Henry' – like Yoni and Dick – and where the water tempts you in coves and tidal lakes and lithe figures already ogled by Matisse. Yet there was joy in it, even as dank as the city became when clouds were grey. Who, in November or December this far north in the northern hemisphere, could defeat such early dark in a glance. And so what if he'd never get invited to Bellagio – and what exactly was waiting for him in Dubai? A thousand cushions? The sand was more gritty along Sandymount than at the Velvet Strand. This he remembered palpably, from the bottom of each foot on up to that spot at the base of the neck that seems to have a micro stretched cord of invisible viscous – a string tightened to the note – how smooth that Velvet Strand was when he was there with Nuala the first time. The dunes came down like valets with special towels; the dunes themselves: lounge chairs and sensuous creatures napping between hot and cool. He considered the little people and Jonathan Swift's fate: not bad; open-mouthed, a loud choir of one man ringing, *Words, words! Language!* like these syllables and characters were atoms of our flesh to be outspoken in whatever sense existing made us. He was buried as a saint and yet he was a sensible man. It was possible to be sensible and saintly, Denny observed, but so often people considered these terms absolute. What about Madonna, Lady Gaga, the teen Lorde, or if there were an artist to come named by industry: Absolute Sainte Whore? What if she were Sans Whore or Sans Heure? It didn't matter, except it mattered to some who are commissioned to license appropriateness. 'Saint Swift laid feet in both worlds, made "appropriateness" his bed,' Nuala explained to Denny, as if she was willing to defend this thesis in front of Denny or in front of a committee. 'You can call me parochial but I've always been open-minded,' she said, grinning at Den'.

He liked thinking about Nuala when he remembered how they laughed walking through the tall grassy dune entrance at Portmarnock. They'd been looking at the CartaGridz site the night before, trying to identify eddies and sandbars – and then they were both caught realising how anatomical the coast appeared – like Como. Wide eyes and smiles grew. They knew what the other was thinking. The night prevailed in a hail of outlandish giggles followed by a swarm to the eyes of bar and eddy. He'd had almost as much fun with Kath, and certainly the Saint and Sarge could get him laughing and thinking about similar allusions. But in Nuala's voice, a softer version of Denny's, and from the velvet hospitality of her parochial curiosities, the sheets had something on sand – although sand would do fine. They laughed going through the tufts, reminded of how physical everything was to them. They weren't tripping. They were clutching earth while reaching for stars they'd never need to know the names of. They felt strongly planted, young as they really were, and when they yearned to go anywhere, to *be* anywhere, they hankered. They were obsessed by a faint pervasive awareness of the popularity of things around them, of whims, and their own making; so they followed this adrenalin muted – like a single informed volume under a light veil of gauze – to be read.

Even Sarge's soft hex, 'A sphinx on every house!' (instead of pox, the teaser!), was a welcome way of saying goodbye. It was '*good* bye' in a grand manner, in the way passengers – steerage or first-class – set sail on future *Titanic*s whose voyages and voyagers would redeem a sense of the transcendence for all travellers, ill-fated or graced. When he left for Nigeria, the dull green of his uniform was at least sharp and smooth and clean; and this reassured Sarge's friends, who had never seen him in his 'uni' – only from pictures on his phone, telling them he'd be all right. Sharp, smooth, clean. In a way this was not Sarge at all, and in a way it absolutely was. And although he was not going to the land of the Ancient Egyptians, at least he was going to Africa. 'Sphinx' had become a bit of craic. 'Up your sphinx with rubber minks!' Sarge was keen to say whenever he disbelieved something.

'You mean *minx*?' the Saint added, elevating the table to a collective 'Whoooah!'

Denny had to hand it to him: maybe the Saint didn't always say what was on his mind, but what was on his mind was usually at least somewhat provocative. To Sarge's rubber-minks remarks, Kath would usually retort – as though she was uninterested – 'Don't bother!' . . . stringing out the '*bah*-ther' almost like a bleat. Then she'd move in for the strike, saying 'Save them for yourselves' – emphasising her observation that Sarge must have multiple personalities to say something so stupid. Of course they were all in for the craic, and the ribbing was part of the call-and-response they'd come to enjoy from each other. Sarge, no dummy, would sometimes look Kath deep in her eyes and say, '*Bah*-ther; that sounds a good deal like "maybe"' – which it is in Irish, and was possibly true for Kath. She certainly had a fun side. And to Nuala's schooling Kath's was much more *street*, so if Nuala was open to amusement, you knew Kath would be triple the effect – even if she acted the righteous part. She could be, in her feminist persuasion, the darling defence of conscious acts. Against bigotries, Kath had decided the punks were slightly more activists than the anarchists. To tease, Sarge would hold his hand as a peace-sign downward and with the middle finger of his other hand 'sign it' – to bar the 'A'.

'I'm not that, and you know it, Sarge!' Kath would shout. Then she'd flick her peace-sign up and cross her index finger over it and run it like a saw, as if to say – in a friendly way – *screw you*.

People say hello and goodbye in the oddest ways. It's like that scene from the musical where everyone has their own special little farewell handshake. There was nothing wrong with the craic ('Only if it becomes a cancer,' Naula's father would say). What was wrong was when you didn't say a thing and you wanted to.

Chapter Forty Six

He'd smelt the salt; both Denny and the Saint had. The only confluence was that they had – and Denny would think about it again now. The breeze and the ocean were the same as on the day when Denny held on to the earth with both hands, fingernails digging in just for a moment to see what it would be like to adhere to a cliff. He wondered if he'd ever be weak enough or sad enough to give in to the feeling below, but his brain shuddered with the thought. How the breeze lifted the dandelions so that Denny could recall summer, and the skin of shins, warmed cotton, laughter spreading through his face as the boy lay elongated in the grass of western Ireland. He wondered what it would be like to cling a little less and let the wind tuck under him. He'd feel the cool slippery steel of the air's fingers lift him upward as though he were some seagull, hovering without exertion, and then an unexpected gust sent him sailing at an impossible angle, as though he were on an amusement ride. Realising he was too late, his own amusement vanished and the edge of the country he sought to adopt; the marvel of coastline became lost to the scrim at the back of his eyes. He could snap out of the bad daydream but it was too late to have dreamed it.

Denny turned in the direction of where he imagined Galway bay would be and found a tune for his head. Even across the width of the country he could be compelled to be someplace other than where he was. How was this? Why? What compelled him to be in more than one place at once? Then he heard a voice from the end of the bar in Brownington, 'Who's the old man in the corner?' Denny was in the shadows but still

177

a single light, a bulb from the far end of the bar's mirror, showed the impression of a young man turned old too soon. He did and he didn't want to be that person. Would there be a Kathy Ireland in his future? There would be a Kath and a Nuala but he couldn't be sure of it then. He carefully rose and shook off the crumbs from his pants and jacket and stepped up onto the secure part of the field that wasn't such a hazard. As he looked over the waves coming in like squadrons of furrowed old men's eyebrows, he laughed to himself. He heard Kath, as in a wet warm whisper in his ear, bringing him to along the canal: 'You can cry about the prospect but you could have cried about the prospect at any time.' Kath was usually the most wise about these things, even if the way she put words to a friend was hard to hear. He remembered what he'd said to her as they waited at the centre of the bridge at Portobello: 'In a few days it would have been the Saint's birthday.'

'It *is* the Saint's birthday, Den'.' She meant a birthday is a birthday whether you're still around to celebrate or gone. 'And gone isn't gone any more, is it?' Kath hammered in a little more. 'Maybe he's on C-85, for fuk's sake, Denny.' She meant the comet that had lately been in the news.

'I doubt much of anything's living on C-85,' Denny said. He was looking straight down into the centre of the canal and Kath was looking out ahead, fixing her gaze at a quarter of a mile beyond where the water swirled under Denny's nose.

'There's a bit of ocean in this here canal, Denny,' Kath stated.

'*Sea*. But call it what you will.'

'You're testin' my Spanish now, are you, Den'?'

'Yes, *si*, my good friend . . . ' Denny was teasing and this was a good thing.

Denny continued, 'I suppose everyone we ever knew and then a few we didn't could be up there – though probably not on any *comet*.'

'No, you're right. Mud and ice never made much for anybody – except fun for a whole lot of kids,' Kath confirmed. Then she added, as if to appease him: 'Well, no matter what, he wasn't going to be Mister Ambassador Big of Big Smoke. We know that.'

Denny was taken aback because he'd never heard Kath so adamant about what the Saint could or couldn't have become. It was enough just to be *golden*, Denny thought. Yet the Saint did have a 'Mr Ambassador Big' sort of way about him, thin as he was. Slender as he was, he lived big, and if he didn't have a swagger to match, he sure had a long stride. People liked him and he fit right in, never even trying. There was no earthly reason why he couldn't be someone's ambassador, or why he wouldn't be big in the eyes of those who would see him in his soft, velveteen, action.

'Larger than life go the dead,' Kath said. This sounded like something her grandmother would say. *Larger than life go the dead.* But it was true. Kath was a natural for the truth.

'Maybe he's up there with a toggle,' said Denny. 'Too many coincidences, coinky-dinks,' he added. And it was the case that there had been a good many coinky-dinks.

'Up there, ah. Up there,' repeated Kath, imagining the Saint up there with a X-Box the size of Texas, 'putting little things in front of us he thinks we may need,' Kath says in disbelief – though she very well might believe it.

'We look up, we do . . . ' acknowledged Denny, as if to prove to Kath that they might not be mad. 'Why else would we if we didn't . . . ' He let himself trail off. He wasn't sure he believed any of the 'up there' business. But he did think the Saint with a toggle added up.

'Still, he wasn't the type to lock himself in his room like a 24/7 gamer. There'd be no earthly reason now but – '; just then he heard Nuala's voice in his other ear. Another hot, moist whisper; Denny appreciated that Nuala could be a magnet to the transcendental at vespers, reminding him in no uncertain terms, 'Denny, like algebra I'm rational at the root' (her sort of come-on line representing her love of maths, a prudent and restrained upbringing, and her obviously covert calculations in the realm of seduction and patience). She was the spice that others said Kath was on the outside, only for Nuala her interior monologue ran more wild – the difference between the sacred bell and the holy smoke.

'There are a whole lot of stars in the sky,' Nuala said, to make a welcoming space for the obvious.

'Yes,' replied Denny. 'But I'm not used to talking to the dark,' he said, peering into the dark of Nuala's eyes.

'You? You once told me you were "King of the Dark".'

'The "King of the Dark" preferred not to talk to the dark. How's that, Nulee?' Denny replied. 'Besides, I was quoting someone.'

'An' who that *someone* be?' Nuala pushed. 'A wee potter doing battle with words?'

'You had me at *wee*,' Denny countered. 'There are a lot of places a person could go . . . . In the dark, I mean.'

'Are you asking or are you tellin', because you're making your way to the slophouse with that blather. Everything leads to everything,' Nuala said.

'*Else*,' added Denny, as if he wanted to propose conditions – like 'Else I'm going home, else we're gonners, else I quit.' He wanted to know what else had happened to the Saint. Else where'd he go? Else what would he have done had he lived to see his golden years turn green? Better yet, how would Denny and the Saint have tightened their friendship, away from the leisure centre, away from the girls at Bray, away from envy and trips Denny realised he'd been left out of, to figure things out on his own? How, across this time in which two friends grow and then grow up, would they find the best ways to remain friends through each other's weddings, kids to come, careers that would surely take them in different directions. Most important, why could this future be for the two of them, one presumably still 'golden' and the other as dark as . . .

He didn't finish his thought because he knew it would loop back to Nuala's point about the night and Denny swearing he wasn't used to talking to the dark. A lie. A sweet lie. Nuala knew it was a lie, of course, because Denny meant it only to tease. He'd gotten through his darks. He found ease in his new neighbourhood along the Dodder. He loved the layers of love he discovered like the geological record with Nuala. And because he wasn't so sure where else he could go, he found peace here. He knew Sarge had gone to Nigeria and wasn't sure when, or even if, he'd be coming back. He was certain he'd remain good pals with Kath until the last of their years – but, still, he couldn't imagine the day when Kath would be 'gone'. Even just knowing she was a few blocks from the city centre allowed that Kath was always present. Of course she was. Half of Denny's conscience was Kath's, it seemed to him, like the voice that just won't go away. And even when the voice was a nuisance, he appreciated its concerned companionship. Where Mick went and the seven Marys (Denny assumed he met along the way at least seven Marys) was also not 'gone'; Mick would *go* but he never would *let go*. Not that Michael Anthony let go. But where do the living go from here? Denny had had time to think about it and yet the answer was *rain*. He'd come a long way, he had: a visitor, now a settler; he'd be a friend to Ireland, even if Ireland's name were only Nuala, or Dodder, or a chalky hand at Listons or the manager at Clerys. He'd be the new century's heartbeat to the stones beneath the floor at Saint Patrick's. He'd be skin, where skin matters, to the mask of a patriarch. He'd be Brian Ború in another foreign accent, from the clan of some unlikely waywards charmed by the Claddagh, and if only eyes would have met him as they rushed into the black chapel of the Big Smoke, St Marys, or around that curve in Galway – 'Call her "Oyster Girl",' Sarge teased Den. Brian Ború the stud or dog or pub; Brian Ború the harp beneath your pelvis, a constant skipping Elvis, the tip of the needle a woman or man just wants to scratch; for all cures and incapacities, her inhabitancy Herbig-Haro 110', shimmer-shimmer dew; waters running free and round what any brass plug like a rhino was heavy inside to stop. He'd be the wave curling at Strandhill and the sand at Sandymount. Surely an eye would smile to see him.

How lucky he was for his adult life to have begun in Rathmines inside the narrow black door that looked like the entrance to a gnome's coffin, understating modesty beside a Georgian red beauty. It was like a smudge more than a prick, coal and dreck in the mouth of a French kiss, while next door the candy-apple-lipped model wore her glossy purchase like a spigot and purse, stepping out into the sunshine that made everyone smell her honeyed perfume and experience a hot wind torque and seize now, along the street, by the kiln of her stride. He had read Mohan's reports about the discovery of a half-rhino-half-stallion and he knew why the lads had placed the rhino in the Dodder. 'Up the invader of the river with rhino!' Like a black door among holiday lights, stealth trumped wealth – except when you needed the other. Still, what luck to have existed as he did in Rathmines, even as the Tiger lost its roar. And to be so unwanted, invisible most times . . . maybe it allowed him to grow up. Or, more like, better like the cosmic dance: he was meeting the curves newly, 'better late than never' – and in his case, *now, late and ever*.

Nuala said, 'somewhere between Eta Carinae and Corvus; this could be your Saint at ease.' It seemed just the point Kath would make, too. And Sarge would endorse it, although with a '*Hmpf,*' and a shrug. There was nothing saying the Saint couldn't be moving his glory in the star-power of three hundred million light-years away.

'He had somewhere to go,' provided Nuala. 'He wouldn't miss a beat,' Denny said to the air, and he snapped his fingers.

The rhinos had marched up to the skirts of the Himalayas. The big wide world wouldn't remain frozen forever. Clouds lifted with bells. Mist replaced the covering of their skins. What fossils they would leave when they were through were bone enough for someone else's future. There was a cascade of language neither Nuala nor Denny understood, neither Sarge nor Mick nor Kath, but maybe the Saint now. Then again, Denny wasn't sure he believed in any of this. 'Any of *this*,' Nuala emphasised for him, holding out her hand; her palm uplifted. The trek from Madras to the mountains, from glaciers' tented flags to the holy fought-through mecca where bleeding hearts divided like new forms over contention; the deserts and the seas, the evolution of pipes and strings, the bump and the forehead; the fore, the before and the foreshadow and forward heave. Where'd the rhino go? I'll tell you, Denny says, the rhino goes where the rhino knows. And the waters around, Nuala adds, the waters round spread tiny galaxies where your hands can touch, where your seat and 'your soul' cool and collect on a hot day; where the big sea enters the Big Smoke and combines with evergreen drop from above the stony towers of Glendalough; where Gulf Stream plants palm around the britches of Wolfe Tone in Bantry, go figure; to the causeways, to the causes, ahead to the head – which is sometimes the point, into the inlets as outlets, across and through the barriers that no longer breed hate; to the golden dog and the reeds as brotherly, sisterly, tales; lee. But you look at the red dust forged into unimagined space, and you shoot back the distance of millions of generations, and, fuck, feck, fuck – whatever – if there isn't a swirl that looks like a girl's curl; the little sea, unseen, but you'll see it now as the finger bends around the block that was ice – and finds the bone. The boomerang the size of a match-tip; smaller; 'Times Square in someone else's underwear,' Sarge said; the fireside to a next time; the shape that infinity sign makes, orgasmic bow-tie; the deft hand scattering chalk along Listons' blackboard, crumbs; the light on shiny leather shoes and marble eyes and knees at Clerys; the gravestone ahead of horses; constant passing-by. The rim of Nuala's weekend dress long past her First Communion, for the shockingly cold cufflinks – drooping Denny's cloth sleeve – adding tickle to the bull, pulling lobes of palms like ears to where time is made; to the centre of things, blasting core fissuring like the ends of trees, sustained notes radiating everywhere making everything to the touch sensitive and ignited with contact; a button, a button, who's got a button; slime on the moon-snail's exposed reaching foot; the moon's penetration into the colder creatures of earth; foolhardy, the cells of motion sensing catastrophe – sentient, insatiable; earth and all around it grasped in one hand, in the internal eye of the Nuala and Kath and Mick and Sarge and Denny and the Saint and all others you encounter, experiencing individually the clump of grass held onto, the breeze a breath, between the fingers here, and there – the best of it – for another day and another hour.

Denny picked up a stone, dry to the touch, along the river's edge. For something solid, it sure felt light. 'Even what little weight is left is enough to be remembered,' he told himself in the echo of a voice that sounded like the Saint's. He remembered Kath telling him about the myth of the hag: 'It is the people you'll love,' the hag taught. Everyone's beautiful at one time or another. *But the only beauty is love*, Denny thought. He loved the Dodder, he loved the rhino, he had loved his life in Rathmines despite his student poverty and a poverty of luck. He missed the Saint but he still had Kath, the others, and Nuala especially. The stone's weight felt like a thought. Not big enough for a fist, not heavy enough to be a newborn anything, he left it where he found it. It was time to think about dinner, time to play grown-up for yet another night. It was time to do something with Nulee. Give Kath a ring. Send a message to Sarge. Wish upon a star. Command the saints to keep on winning. Live like you've already died and each new hour's an opportunity. Thank your lucky stars. 'Be grateful, you lucky bastard,' Denny said to the air, extending his arm across the first few feet of water.